Travels W

Book One

By Dee Hazelridge

Copyright

Text copyright @ 2016 Dee Hazelridge

All Rights Reserved

Dedication

For Lorraine & Mum

With thanks for their constant love and encouragement

And for Dad

Truly missed

About the Author

Dee Hazelridge has lived all her life in the South East of England. She presently lives in Kent with her partner and numerous, pampered pets!

Although she has been writing for over ten years, Travels With My Aunt is her first published novel.

Preface

When escorting an elderly relative to the sea-side, Katherine Rider finds her quiet life becoming a rollercoaster of emotion and revelation. She soon discovers unwelcome secrets of the past which are likely to change her future.

Her aunt, a self-centred and dictatorial woman, is determined to have her own way in all things, including the choice of a husband for poor Katherine, but Katherine's heart is quickly captivated by a gentle and compassionate new friend who, for a while, brings sunshine into her topsy-turvy world.

Part one of a light-hearted and humorous story concerning the ups and downs of chaperoning elderly people on holiday.

Reviews

Just finished reading Travels with my Aunt by Dee Hazelridge which will be out on Kindle soon. Very amusing story. Lucky enough to have had a preview. Look out for it! You won't be sorry. Made me laugh. Everyone has an aunt like it!

R. Heartland

***

I could relate to the characters because they reminded me of people in my own life. The story isn't rushed, thus making it easier to get to know the characters. Considering the age difference, Katherine dealt with her aunt's outbursts of ill humour exceedingly well. The story also impressed me for its humour, twists and turns. A very satisfying read.

E. Ridgley

***

A very enjoyable and humorous read. I was hooked right from the start and disappointed when it finished... I wanted more! Can't wait for the next book. An excellent, light-hearted read.

L. Pierce

***

I found the story to be an amusing rollercoaster of emotions. I liked the characters because I have known someone just like the aunt. I would recommend this story because it's an easy and enjoyable read.

P. Allen

***

Dee Hazelwood's book 'Travels with my Aunt' is an intriguing, twist of a tale that keeps you on the edge of your seat. An enjoyable read that you won't put down until finished.

S. Sayers

Chapter 1

"Just a moment, Katherine! What are you packing that thing for?" Aunt Phoebe asked, looking over the top of her gold rimmed spectacles.

Her small piggy-eyes glared at me as I clutched my lap-top bag; pulling it protectively to my breast, like a mother might her new-born infant.

"Well, I... I want to keep up with the outside world." I explained, feebly.

"There's nothing going on out there that we need worry about." Aunt Phoebe growled, eyeing the case suspiciously. "Put it back in the cupboard dear."

"But Aunt Phoebe!" I protested. "I have my work to do and how will I be able to..."

My words faltered. What I had intended to say was, 'How can I keep in touch with Jilly without my beloved lap-top?' We had agreed to do so via Skype, morning and night; without my lap-top, how would I cope?

"What's that?" She replied sharply, cupping her knobbly hand to her ear. "Speak up, girl! I can't hear you!"

I swallowed and spoke again.

"I have my work to attend to."

"I'm not taking you along so you can work! I'm taking you along with me so you might find a young man."

At this point, I gulped.

"No man will be interested in a girl whose nose is perpetually stuck to a computer-thingy!" She continued; pointing her finger at my laptop as if it had the plague.

"Aunt Phoebe, I'm not interested in finding a man." I said, following the elderly lady as she shuffled off into her bedroom. "You see... it's like this..."

"Oh, I know what it's like, believe me, dear." She muttered as she popped a bottle of lavender water into a toilet bag.

"You do?" I replied perplexed.

"Oh yes! You fear the sex."

I spluttered at this point. She looked back at me like a teacher who was just about to scold a thirteen-year-old child who'd giggled at the word 'erection' in class.

"Aunt Phoebe... It's got nothing to do with sex!"

"Of course it has! Everything in life is to do with sex... at your age, anyway. It's the perpetual evil which blights our lives." She announced, clearly and concisely.

"No, what I mean to say is..."

"You have to get over this fear of 'the penis'..." She suggested seriously. "Or you'll never get a man."

Once again, I spluttered, but this time, turning my face to the wall.

"I don't know why you appear so shocked, Katherine. Mind you, I blame your mother! She was never one to comprehend the 'facts of life'. If she'd explained a little more to you when it mattered, you might not be in the situation that you are now... without a man."

"But you've got it all wrong..." I tried to explain.

"Katherine! I will not be contradicted! I am a woman of the world and I understand these things."

"But Aunt Phoebe, I'm thirty-six years old. I don't want a man! I don't need a man!"

"Rubbish! Every woman wants a man of her own and a child of her own. You're not getting any younger, you know."

I was beginning to feel irritated by her continuous references to my advancing years.

"Its time you settled down and raised a family."

This time I howled with laughter. Through my tears, I could see my Aunt's beady eyes staring back at me... dangerously.

"And what, may I ask, is so funny about that?"

Her arms were folded across her corseted-bosoms.

"Aunt Pheobe! For the last time, I'm not into men... I like women!"

Her eyes narrowed.

"Katherine, having only female friends in your life will not steer you in the right direction to finding a suitable man... unless one of your lady friends has an eligible gentleman friend or brother whom she might introduce you to. Having continuous fun with 'the girls' is all very well, but take it from me; they won't keep you warm in bed on a cold winter's night." She advised, with knowing wink.

"I beg to differ, Aunt. I've known plenty of girls who have done just this."

"The young girls with whom you shared a bunk at the Sunday school camps when you were ten years old, may have had to huddle together to keep warm, but you are a little too old now for those sorts of frolics. Now, give me a hand with my suitcase, will you dear?"

I had the dubious duty of escorting my eighty-six-year-old aunt to the coast for her annual romp. (Up at seven thirty and a stroll along 'the front' before breakfast. Luncheon at twelve thirty sharp. Forty-winks in a deck-chair after lunch in partial shade, but out of the wind. Afternoon tea at three thirty and the evening meal at six o'clock. A couple of hours of 'whist' commencing at seven thirty, and lights out by ten.) Phew! What an exhausting itinerary... One which was repeated daily during her stay in the same hotel, same room - in fact, the same dreary old routine every year.

My sister, Anna and I would fight over who might have the honour of relaying Aunt Phoebe to her 'watering hole', playing nurse-maid, companion, card partner or opponent, chauffeur and general dogs-body. This year, I had drawn the short straw and I can still see my sister's smug face as she grinned from ear to ear.

"Never mind dear..." Mum whispered quietly. "You'll get your reward in Heaven."

But I wanted my reward now! I wanted to be with Jilly who, as I speak, was travelling to Dublin for a wild weekend with the rest of the gang... including that leggy blonde who won't leave Jilly alone. I frowned as I thought of my Jilly; alone, and at the mercy of that blonde... And without me there to keep an eye on proceedings. It's not that I don't trust Jilly... It's just that she's... Well, let's not even go there. I trust Jilly; or at least....

"Well, take it!" Aunt Phoebe barked, intruding on my thoughts.

"Sorry Aunt." I replied, dutifully taking her suitcase.

I packed the remaining luggage in my car, including my laptop, and waited patiently as instructions were fired at an obliging neighbour who was entrusted with the care of 'Tiddles'; my Aunt's cat. When the neighbour was in no further doubt of her requirements, Aunt Phoebe waved her stick in the air and instructed me to "make tracks!"

Chapter 2

As we journeyed towards the coast, I glanced at my Aunt who had become strangely silent. Instead of giving me the benefit of her vast experience in road travel, (a bus ride taken once a week to visit my cousin Shirley in Croydon) it had all become too much for her and she had allowed herself to be lured into the arms of Morpheus. I smiled; glad that at least the last forty-five minutes of the journey would be conducted in some peace and quiet, allowing me to think about my life.

I always thought about my life when I was with Aunt Phoebe. I suppose she spent so many hours nagging me about my inadequacies, that in the end, I too, began to seriously doubt my purpose in life. Her constant reminders of the years slipping by without having bagged a 'decent' chap, and given him countless children were certainly a cause for concern. Well, it was for at least thirty seconds! Time and time again, Mum had tried to explain to Aunt Phoebe that as a lesbian, I had no interest in men whatsoever. Huh! Fat lot of good it always did. Mum explained that my partner, Jilly, was as near as I would ever get to a man; a remark which had, at the time, made me snort in amusement. Aunt Phoebe had frowned, but remained in blissful ignorance of my lot in life.

"She'll grow out of it!" She informed Mum with confidence... each Christmas.

So, Jilly was looked upon as my 'best friend' who accompanied me everywhere, except on holiday with Aunt Phoebe; this I had to endure alone.

"She's your family, Kat... I don't need to be involved in this."

I can remember feeling a little hurt. She knew that I hated 'fun at the coast with Aunt Phoebe' but instead of coming along to support me, had arranged a weekend away with some friends, including 'the blonde'!

"Take a book to read." She had suggested with an indifferent wave of her hand. "The time will fly and you won't miss me, one little bit."

Hmmm...

I pulled into the car park of The Hotel Vista which faced the sea. Aunt Phoebe was still in the land of nod, snoring gently and I sighed with relief. At least I would be able to check-in without the usual fuss.

"Good afternoon, Madam... May I be of assistance?"

Hellooo! A new face on the reception desk - and pretty too!

"Good afternoon. My name is Katherine Rider. My Aunt, Mrs. Hawkins and I are booked-in for a week of 'fun and games'" I advised; an eyebrow raised in irony.

The pretty receptionist grinned back at me; her eyes sparkling. My heart gave a little quiver and I cleared my throat; ashamed of the pleasure her face was providing.

"Is your aunt with you?" The receptionist asked, glancing over my shoulder in wonder.

"Yes, but she's asleep in the car – thankfully!" I grinned.

"She can't be that bad, surely?"

"Well, I hate to disillusion you so soon, so maybe I'll just allow you to make up your own mind when I bring her in."

"O-kay... Now you're beginning to worry me." She grinned.

Wow! What a lovely smile.

Suddenly, a rather flustered looking man came rushing into the hotel lobby.

"Has anyone lost an Aunt?" He cried.

"Oh Lord! That's my cue!" I cried, hastily signing the register and handing back the pen.

"Need any help?" She volunteered.

"That would be perfect." I replied, thankfully.

I smiled my best smile, just for her. I used to practice this one in front of the mirror when I was first seeing Jilly. Evidently it worked, not just for Jilly, but also the receptionist, for she closed her book quickly and trotted around the desk to join me in capturing my escapee relative.

Christina, the pretty receptionist, was charm itself to Aunt Phoebe. When we had 'rounded-up' Aunty, Christina took her gently by the arm and very slowly, guided her to the lobby entrance, speaking of recent weather conditions in the area and advising that it was roast beef for dinner. Aunt Phoebe smiled and looked as pleased as punch. Christina pointed out the beautiful, yellow chrysanthemums which she had picked from her mother's garden and placed with pride in the hotel lobby, and how she would take great pleasure in picking some more, especially for Aunt Phoebe's bedroom.

This young lady certainly had a way about her!

I found it hard to take my eyes off Christina. It wasn't that she was tall, slim and elegant like Jilly... No, she was about my own height, well-covered, but not fat, and had the most wonderful blue eyes, which sparkled like diamonds when she smiled. I physically had to pinch myself as a reminder that I was already 'spoken for' and the chances of Christina being remotely gay were pretty slim!

Christina carried up the excess baggage which I couldn't manage, and soon Aunt Phoebe was comfortably ensconced in an arm chair with a 'nice cup of tea' and a sea view from her bedroom window.

"Now, is there anything else I can get for you, Mrs. Hawkins?" The receptionist asked.

"No dear. You've been extremely kind already and I'm sure we are holding you up from your duties." My Aunt replied; smiling graciously. "And Katherine, here, can find the way to her own room!" She said, glancing at me in disapproval.

I swallowed uncomfortably.

"That's fine then. All cosy now."

Christina smiled up at me and winked. My heart nearly exploded!

"Well, I'll leave you ladies to unpack and I'll see you at dinner."

I walked with Christina to my Aunt's bedroom door.

"I can't thank you enough for all your help." I said, wishing I could find something else to say to keep her talking for a little longer.

"It was my pleasure."

"You seem to have charmed my Aunt."

"I have several of my own. They are all unique in their own special way! See you at dinner."

"Yes. Thanks again." I called as she walked down the corridor.

"No worries." She replied.

Wow! My heart beat rapidly and my knees began to buckle beneath me... Until Aunt Phoebe yelled out my name!

Chapter 3

I knocked for Aunt Phoebe at five thirty as instructed. It would give us a full half hour to enjoy a pre-dinner sherry before launching into roast beef and two veg. As we walked down the staircase, I could smell the aroma of vegetables. I turned up my nose but the gesture had been caught by my Aunt's sharp eye.

"It's all good, honest food, Katherine. And the smell of cauliflower is certainly a welcome change from that cheap smelling scent you have been wearing all day!"

Well, there's nothing like telling you straight!

"It happens to be a very expensive French perfume!" I pointed out.

"More fool you for paying good money for rubbish!"

Jilly had given it to me on my last birthday. Jilly had impeccable taste and liked me to smell tasteful too.

"After all honey, you care bugger-all about your looks and dress; at least if you smell respectable, I won't feel so embarrassed when we are out!" She'd giggled; squeezing my bottom affectionately.

Jilly could be very physical at times, which was always nice, but her tongue could be a little cutting too.

"Well, I'm sorry if it offends you, Aunt. I'll go easy on it from now on."

"What's wrong with just soap and water, I'd like to know? Or perhaps a little dab of '4-7-11' behind your ears?"

I must admit, I did agree with my Aunt on this one, but I liked to please Jilly as much as possible and if wearing the perfume of her choice is what she wanted, then, wear it I would!

A waitress showed us to our table in the dining room. Having been to the same hotel for the past sixteen years, my Aunt was well acquainted with the location of her regular table, but she still enjoyed the pomp and ceremony of being escorted to the white damask covered table, each evening.

With my Aunt comfortably seated, and perusing the wine menu, I took my opportunity to look about me in hopes of catching sight of Christina. Of course, it was possible that Christina had finished work and gone home to enjoy a nice Saturday evening with some lucky bloke! I wondered what he was like; dark or fair, tall and muscular or perhaps small and slim.

I suddenly noticed a man sitting a few tables away. As our eyes met, he raised his glass to me and silently wished me a good evening. I smiled in return.

"You could do worse than him, dear." Aunt Phoebe observed.

"I'm sorry?"

"He's here every year and is very comfortably off."

"Aunt! He's as old as Methuselah! And besides that, I'm not interested in men!"

Aunty huffed and continued to scrutinize the menu. Suddenly, the dining room door opened and Christina walked in wearing a stunning trouser and waistcoat suit. The blouse beneath was silky and low cut, and very sexy. I could feel the saliva slithering down my chin as I stared.

"Katherine! Close your mouth, dear! That gentleman will not think much of you catching flies like that!"

I quickly looked at my Aunt and then at the gentleman. He continued to smile and even winked, which caused me to blush. I gulped and cleared my throat.

"Please Aunt! I'd rather you didn't make comments like that!" I hissed, hiding my face beneath the menu.

"Good evening, Mrs. Hawkins and Miss. Rider. I take it you are both settled in now?" Christina asked as she stood before us. "Can I take your order for wine?"

I opened my mouth, intending to order a favourite wine of Jilly's, when Aunty interposed and ordered something rather less flamboyant and certainly more modest in price.

Christina dutifully took down the order, but before departing, she looked under her eyelashes at me and smiled such a smile that made me long to touch her soft cheek.

Good Lord! What was wrong with me? Here was I, a very fortunate woman, already in a relationship with the most elegant creature I know and certainly envied by most of our friends, gay or otherwise. I was often told how lucky I was, even though I was already aware of this. Jilly and I had met at a dinner party given by a mutual friend some years before. The attraction was instantaneous... well, for me, anyway. After the party, whenever we happened to meet, I found myself following her around like a puppy or a very willing slave. She obviously enjoyed the attention and even joked with her close friends, how I would do anything she requested; and I would have! Sadly, Jilly's Mother died and Jilly pushed away all her trendy friends but strangely enough, allowed me closer to her; confiding her deepest thoughts and taking every ounce of love and care which, I was so willing to bestow on her.

I moved into Jilly's flat and my happiness was complete. We'd spend hours talking, laughing and making love on her King-size bed with the baby-pink satin sheets. I thought I had died and gone to Heaven! But inevitably, time helped to heal her grief and though still a little anxious at times, started to venture back out into the real world, dragging me willingly behind her, like a security blanket for when things got tough. But as time passed, the special bond between us seemed to crumble, and more often than not, Jilly did things by herself. I was pleased that she had found her confidence again, but sad that my constant love was no longer required. So, this is how our life together has been for the past two years. But I was still a very lucky girl.

Then why was I so attracted to Christina?

Chapter 4

I watched Christina walk away from our table; fascinated how her hips swayed gracefully from side to side.

"Oh my God!" I sighed.

"What was that, dear?"

"I-I said I'll go the hole-hog... and order cheese and biscuits this evening." I muttered, covering my tracks.

"Too much cheese will add pounds to your figure, Katherine."

"Yes... Well, I'll bear that in mind, Aunt." I muttered casting another hungry glance in Christina's direction.

She was busy pouring wine into glasses and then placed them on a silver tray before returning to our table. As she approached, our eyes met and I'm sure I saw a flicker of something in her blue orbs.

"Here we are ladies." She said, carefully placing each glass on the table.

"Thank you my dear. I'm most obliged to you." Aunty simpered.

"My pleasure, Mrs. Hawkins. Has Maria taken your order for a starter yet?"

The last part of the question was aimed at me.

"Err, no not yet."

"I'll hurry her along."

"There's no rush!" I replied hastily as she turned away.

She looked back, a little surprised.

"What I mean to say is… we're quite comfortable just… sitting here… and…"

I was lost for words. I'd said the first thing which came into my head; anything to delay Christina from walking away from me."

"Well, there's no rush, that's all."

"Okay." Christina said, smiling that wonderful smile again.

Oh dear! I was getting-in deeper and deeper and right under Aunt Phoebe's nose!

"What are you babbling on about, Katherine! Of course we are waiting for the waitress to take our order and I would be obliged, Christina dear, if you can hurry her along. I intend to play whist this evening and I would prefer my dinner to be settled before I retire to bed."

I closed my eyelids briefly and sighed. This was to be our tedious routine for the next seven dreary evenings and all I wanted was to keep Christina talking for just another few minutes, but Aunty was determined to have her own way as always. I opened my eyes as I heard Christina's next words.

"Mrs. Hawkins, my Aunt Lucy is visiting the hotel this evening; I wondered if you'd allow me to introduce her to you? She is also a keen whist player and I'm sure will be delighted to join you in a game, if agreeable?"

"Oh my dear! How very kind, but I hate to be a burden to anyone, as Katherine here will assure you. But it will be nice to have a fresh opponent. Katherine is all very well, but she plays cards like a five-year-old!"

Christina chuckled; her eyes finding mine. As they met, I stopped breathing. She held my eyes for a few moments, before turning back to my Aunt.

"Well, that's settled and maybe Miss. Rider might like to join me and some of our other residents in the garden for drinks and nibbles at eight?" Christina suggested, turning to me. "It's a new innovation for the summer evenings. There will be some music and fairy lights... Not exactly Monte Carlo, but certainly atmospheric."

The thought of spending an evening with a bunch of strangers didn't really enthral me, but it was the way Christina had made the suggestion - almost a plea! And if she was going to be there... Well...

"I'd be delighted." I smiled back.

"Good!" Christina replied.

"You'd do better staying here to improve your game, Katherine dear, but since it's our first evening, you may as well run along and enjoy yourself."

Well, bully for me!

I glanced at Christina who had the biggest smile on her face.

"Well, I'll go and... chase up that waitress for you." She said, holding the silver drinks tray close to her body.

How I envied that tray!

She gave me another smile and then walked toward the kitchen. My eyes followed her; imploring her to walk a little slower so I could enjoy her lovely figure for just a little longer. Suddenly a tap on the back of my hand brought me back down to earth.

"Katherine, please go and ask that nice gentleman if he would like to join us for coffee after dinner."

"Oh, Aunt Phoebe!" I wailed.

Chapter 5

My Aunt had one eye on her playing cards and the other on her new opponent; Christina's Aunt Lucy. Lucy was of a similar age to Phoebe and though her disposition was somewhat softer than my Aunt's, her brain was just as sharp – just as enquiring.

As the elderly ladies pursed their lips in concentration, I quietly left the comfortable armchair where I had resided since dinner. Glancing at my watch, I noticed it was seven forty-five; fifteen minutes before the other residents and Christina were due to assemble in the garden for the evening's entertainment. I imagined a selection of slightly faded Christmas fairy-lights hanging limply on a red brick wall. A trestle table covered with a floral, plastic cloth (usually reserved for picnics) and a few bottles of

Vino-collapso, precariously perched at one end, alongside some tired sausage rolls and peanuts.

My reasons for agreeing to attend were to avoid Roger Spence; the eligible gentleman whom my Aunt had decided had 'an eye' for me. (And had promised a return visit at eight fifteen to ply me with Crème De Menthe and to explain the wonders of his clay-pipe collection!) My other reason was to spend some more time with the delightful Christina away from my Aunt. I had only seen Christina once more at dinner; she was enjoying a chat with one of the other residents as they were leaving the dining room. I watched her face as she listened with interest to their story; laughing in all the right places and frowning when the moment dictated. She had it down to a fine art! Christina had the most expressive face I had ever seen in a woman and I was determined to capture some of those expressions for myself. Her wonderful smile was already imprinted on my soul and I had only to capture it in my sketchbook to keep as a souvenir when my week here in 'funsville' was over. She did glance once more in our direction – well, I think it was in our direction, but she never returned to our table.

After popping to my bedroom and changing into jeans and a heavy jumper, I made my way to the French doors leading into the garden. As I opened the door, I half expected to hear the hum of voices gathered around the barbeque or singing along to Barry Manilow's rendition of 'I Write The Songs'. But I was surprised to hear only an acoustic guitar playing softly at a little distance.

I could see a glimmer of light at the far end of the terrace and slowly made my way towards it. The evening was surprisingly warm and I wondered if my heavy jumper would be just too much. I could hear one or two birds chirping their night songs to each other and the smell of honey-suckle which adorned the hotel walls, exuded heady-sweet nectar as I sauntered by.

"Hi." Someone said from the shadows.

I jumped and looked in their direction. Several tea-lights were burning, scattered along the rustic stone wall which divided the terrace from the garden, proper. There was no barbeque, no sausage rolls, or peanuts and certainly no Barry Manilow! Just Christina and a bottle of good wine.

"Hey." I replied, waiting for the yell of "Surprise! Surprise!" from other residents hiding secretly in the shrubbery. "Where is everyone?"

Christina rose from some steps which lead down to the immaculately clipped lawn.

"No one else... Just us! I thought you needed an escape, so I provided one." She giggled.

I stood, astonished for a few moments.

"Wine? It's the good stuff – not the rubbish they offer in there." Christina smiled, offering me a glass.

"Thanks. Aren't you supposed to be off duty?" I asked, sitting down on a vacant step.

"Yes, two hours since, but my Aunt has been thrust upon me by my cousin, Judith - Aunt

Lucy's daughter, who at this moment is enjoying a West End show and a swanky weekend away in London. And the thought of having a quiet night in with my doting Aunt gives me the headache! I got the idea when you arrived with your Aunt earlier today. I knew the two old dears would be ideally suited as company and you looked like you needed an ally... I hope I didn't presume?"

"No!" I laughed.

I took a sip of wine and sighed.

"You've been a God-send. My Aunt is very demanding and this holiday is a 'short straw' for me, so even to get away for a couple of hours, is pure bliss." I smiled, gratefully.

Christina smiled too and our eyes lingered for a few moments, until I cleared my throat.

"Have you worked at the hotel, long? I can't remember seeing you here before."

"Long enough." She replied. "My parents own it – have for donkey's years, but I was living abroad until ten months ago. It's a long story, but I've come home with my tail between my legs and I'm working my bed and board."

"Oh dear." I replied, sympathetically. "Do I get the impression that hotel work isn't what you enjoy?"

"Oh Lord, no! I love it!" She enthused. "I managed my own hotel in the south of France; a region called Castagniccia; lots of beautiful mountain villages... Near Corsica. It was wonderful." She said, her mind having drifted for a few moments.

"Why did you leave?" I asked, but immediately regretting the enquiry. "I'm sorry; I'm being too inquisitive."

Her attention returned to me and she smiled.

"No worries. No big secret. My partner and I ran the hotel for about seven years. Unfortunately, Sam got itchy feet and wanted to move to one of the larger resorts. I didn't, so we had a problem. In the end, it drove a nail in the coffin of our relationship. Sam wanted to ship out and I couldn't afford the up-keep of the hotel by myself, so we sold up and I came home."

"I'm sorry." I said, feeling bad for her, but thinking what an idiot Sam must have been. "So, do you plan to stay here indefinitely?"

"Just until I can find a way back. Trouble is; we lost a lot of money when we sold the hotel. Financially, I'm trying to make ends meet. Still, it's not so bad here." She said, glancing around the walls of the hotel garden. "I'm making the best of it."

I remained quiet for a few moments, thinking over her words.

"So, what do you do, Katherine?" She asked, suddenly.

"Call me 'Kat'. Everyone else does... well, except Aunt Phoebe, that is. To her, I am but a child!" I declared, melodramatically.

My new friend smiled.

"I'm an artist." I said, taking a sip of wine and wondering what her reaction would be.

"Wow!" She said, slowly. "What sort?"

"Portraits; people, cats, dogs, hamsters... you name it!" I grinned. "I'm no Leonardo, but I make a living... Just."

Christina stared at me in what I can only describe as 'astonishment'.

"Well, well. It just goes to show; you shouldn't judge a book by its cover." She murmured.

Oh dear! Just what sort of story did my cover portray?

Chapter 6

Christina poured more wine into my glass.

"So, are you working on a picture – sorry, portrait, at the moment?" Christina asked as she carefully placed the bottle onto the step beside her.

"Not exactly." I replied, taking a sip of wine. "I sketch from time to time and that's what I want to do this holiday."

"How wonderful. I wish I was artistic." She replied with a sigh. "There are so many beautiful places around here which I'd love to catch on paper. You must let me show you some."

I mentally gasped; the thought of spending time climbing over rugged rocks or walking miles along a breezy headland to sketch Christina's favourite views, made my heart beat a little faster.

"I...I'd love that... that's if you can spare the time." I stammered.

"Of course. Perhaps tomorrow morning? We can arrange the old ladies' blankets and see that they are comfortable in the conservatory together, then, we can escape!" Christina grinned, mischievously. "What do you say?"

I just couldn't control the huge grin which had appeared on my face.

"I think it's a perfect plan!"

"We'll take a picnic!" Christina announced enthusiastically. "I'll ask the kitchen staff to prepare something nice and I'll pinch a bottle of Father's best red to go with it. You do like red wine, don't you?" She asked hesitantly.

"Oh yes!" I cried. "I drink anything... I mean, I drink red or white."

"Good. How very exciting! It's not often I get to have such fun. I'm glad you've turned up, Katherine." She grinned.

"So am I." I smiled with delight.

There was no word of a lie here. I was glad and grateful to her sparing me the time and providing me with fun. Even if I couldn't touch, I could look upon her beautiful face and think myself lucky... And maybe feel a little sorry for Sam, her ex, who must be the most stupid man on the planet!

The following morning found me walking a little behind Christina as she enthused over distant hills, birds gliding effortlessly on the thermals and the crashing of the ocean against the rocks below.

We had left Aunts Phoebe and Lucy conspiring and gossiping together in a sunny aspect of the hotel conservatory. With cups of tea in hand and crocheted blankets tucked around their respective old knees, we left, but not before a last minute warning from Aunt Phoebe.

"Now, don't take up all of Christina's time, Katherine. She is a busy young woman and no doubt has better things to do than spend time amusing you! Besides, what is the point of you coming on holiday with me if you are not going to be here?" She asked, haughtily.

I glanced; embarrassed, at Christina. Our eyes met and she winked.

"I'm sure we won't be gone that long, Mrs. Hawkins and besides, Aunt Lucy here, says I never get enough fresh air and therefore, is much obliged to Katherine for taking me away for a few hours."

I glanced at Aunt Lucy, but she had not heard her niece's speech. I feared that Christina had used some poet licence to convince my Aunt of the necessity of my prolonged absence from her side.

"Very well, my dear. If you say so."

"You didn't hear a word I just said, did you?" Christina laughed.

I jumped out of my reverie and back into the real world, which just at that moment was Christina and I, alone.

"I'm sorry!" I gasped. "I was thinking about my Aunt. I do hope she won't be too much of a trial for your Aunt Lucy!"

"Good Lord, no!" Christina laughed. "Aunt Lucy can hold her own I can assure you. She's 'old school', just like your aunt. They will be just fine."

We walked on a little further; I was aware that Christina was looking at me and I felt my cheeks flush. Christina laughed and suddenly took my hand.

"You are a funny one. Come on. Don't look so nervous. See... this is my first favourite view!"

She pointed to a headland which jutted out into the ocean. The sun smiled happily upon it whilst the sea sprayed its salt water sparklers in return.

"Isn't it just scrummy?" Christina sighed, taking a deep breath and absorbing the sight.

I couldn't quite make up my mind if it was the view of Christina, with all her exciting beauty or the picturesque headland which made my heart beat a little faster. (Actually, I did know, but I kept pushing the thought to the back of my mind!)

"It's truly wonderful. Can we get a little closer?" I asked hopefully.

"Yes. We'll have to climb down part of this cliff which takes us to a coastal path. It will lead us either to the headland, or part way there - as near as you want, at any rate."

I felt Christina's fingers moving gently in my hand. Every nerve in my body twitched in appreciation at this simple gesture, however innocently offered. I closed my eyes, praying it would never end.

"Just look at that cormorant up there!" Christina said, pointing.

I opened up my eyes and felt her hand tighten in mine.

"Come on. Let's chase it!" She cried.

We ran along the cliff edge until the bird was out of sight. Breathing heavily, I held my stomach muscles with my free hand.

"Out of condition, are we?" Christina laughed, puffing slightly herself.

"Well and truly!" I giggled, between gasps.

I had expected Christina to release my hand, but she didn't! Instead, she led me down some man-made rock-steps to another ledge which was to be our pathway to the beautiful headland.

Chapter 7

The lamb's wool blanket, prickled against my bare legs, making them itch! But what kind of impression would I make on Christina, scratching away, leaving welts from ankles to knees? Instead, I rubbed at my skin vigorously with the palm of my hand, hoping my companion wouldn't notice. She didn't... She was engaged in consuming a juicy nectarine without the aid of a box of tissues or face cloth. Answer me this! How can anyone do this elegantly? However, Christina did. She licked her lips, no doubt savouring the last few drops of nectar and popped the fruit's stone into a waste bag by her side. She turned to me with a wicked grin on her face.

"I love nectarines, don't you?"

Yes, I did love nectarines, but only when I stood over a sink to catch the juice.

"Yes, they are fruits of the Gods." I announced.

"Here." She said, handing over the punnet. "Have one."

"Oh! No! Thank you all the same." I hastily replied, holding up my hand. "I'm quite full."

Christina seemed disappointed.

"But Kat! They are gorgeous! You really should try one... Please?"

How could I refuse? So I smiled my consent and picked out one of the attractive fruits and bit gently into it. Immediately, the juice gushed down my chin.

"Oh bugger!" I cursed, fumbling for a serviette.

"Here! Take this one!" Christina laughed, passing over a paper towel.

I mopped myself up, irritated by my lack of delicacy.

"They can be so messy, can't they?" Christina grinned. "But worth it!"

I smiled, but could already feel the juice drying on my skin. I really needed a wet-wipe or preferably, a bath.

"Yes." I muttered.

Christina laid back comfortably on the blanket – while I hugged my knees and thought about ways to wash, surreptitiously.

"Is there a large age gap between your mother and aunt?" Christina asked, shading her eyes from the bright afternoon sun. "After all, your aunt is pretty old, if you don't mind me saying, but you don't seem old enough to have a mum of your aunt's age."

"There's about a fifteen-year difference." I replied, organising myself with a clean tissue. "I think mum was a mistake – or so Grandad told me!"

As Christina closed her eyes, I took the opportunity to spit on the clean tissue before mopping my sticky face.

"Do you have any brothers or sisters?"

"Yes, I have a sister. We usually take it in turns to bring Aunt Phoebe away – though it seems to be my turn more often than not! This year it was my turn again." I replied dismally.

"Still..." Christina exclaimed; sitting up suddenly. "If it wasn't for dear old Aunt Phoebe, you and I wouldn't be enjoying this lovely afternoon together, would we?"

I gulped. Christina was looking deep into my eyes which, I found, most disarming. I could only reply with a lame smile, but my heart was beating like a manic drummer. Christina laid back again and I took a deep breath. So often, straight women gave signals which were misconstrued by gay women, this is why I found it better not to react. Instead, I took out my sketch book and crayons and began to draw a rough outline of the surrounding cliffs, shoreline and birds which flew overhead. Christina lay perfectly still. I couldn't tell if she dozed or just rested, but all that moved was her ribcage as she breathed in and out... in and out. I shook my head quickly to drag my attention away from her curvaceous torso and continued with my pursuit. After completing one or two rough sketches, I turned over another blank sheet and began the outline of something completely different. I didn't know where I was going with it – my charcoal did the walking, but before long, I found myself half way through a portrait of Christina.

"What are you sketching?" Christina asked suddenly.

I nearly jumped out of my skin.

"Nothing!" I fibbed. "Just some rough sketches of the cliffs."

I quickly closed the pages of my book.

"May I see?"

"No... They're nothing special. Just some old sketches."

"Don't be shy." Christina laughed, scrambling onto her knees and demanding to be gratified.

I reluctantly handed over my etchings and cringed as she started to peruse the pages.

There were other illustrations and doodles in the book; some representations done months earlier during a four-day city break in Florence with Jilly, where we spent a less than romantic vacation arguing over this and that. Finally, we agreed to differ and do our own thing; I spent a blissful few hours each day sketching and enjoying Florentine culture whilst Jilly caught up with an old girlfriend whom she just happened to bump into at the airport upon our arrival.

Christina looked long and hard at one sketch in particular. I shifted uncomfortably, sensing it was my sketch of her, but after a few moments of frowning, she placed the book flat on her legs and looked up at me.

"You know, you have a wonderful talent, Kat. I wish I was half as gifted."

I glanced down at the book and realised she had paused on a page of various sketches of Michelangelo's David.

"But you were frowning." I laughed, taking a gulp of wine.

"I was thinking that you must have got pretty close to his 'bits' to have reproduced them so precisely. Either this or you have a natural aptitude when it comes to men's genitals."

I choked. The wine splattered over my legs as I continued to cough. Christina was up in a moment to thump my back.

"Kat! Are you ok?" She asked anxiously.

My coughing subsided but I continued to laugh.

"What's so funny?"

"You are!" I grinned, wiping my moist nose with a tissue.

"What did I say?"

"Never mind." I replied, reclaiming my sketch book and popping it quickly into my backpack. "Let's clear up here and move on."

Christina was still bemused, but I was happy to close the subject.

Chapter 8

We continued walking along the cliffs, stopping from time to time to admire or exclaim over a view. Christina had walked this stretch on many occasions and though she didn't have quite the same enthusiasm as someone seeing these wonders for the first time, her excitement flourished in guiding and relating vital tit-bits of information which the unseasoned visitor might have missed.

"Your sketch book seems pretty full now!" She grinned as I turned to yet another fresh page.

"When I'm on a roll, I just keep going!" I laughed.

"Can I make an observation?" She asked, tentatively.

"Of course!" I replied.

"You never seem to finish the picture before we move on."

I laughed.

"This is my craft! I may not be an expert in much of life, but with a blank page and pen, I can scribble away – put it down for a while, pick it up later and continue with it. It would be like you taking photographs of all this. The difference being, I just roughly sketch it out and fill in the rest later."

"How marvellous! How do you remember it so well?!"

Jilly always remarked that I must have a photographic memory. Maybe she was right.

"I don't really know – I just do. Things of beauty always make a lasting impression on me – even years later; I close my eyes and there it is! All ready for me to pick up where I left off!"

"Why don't you finish it while you are sitting sketching?"

"Then I would miss all the other delightful prospects!" I replied, gesturing with my arms at the views around me.

"You could take photographs?" Christina suggested.

"I could and I sometimes do, but somehow, the images are flat, whereas my sketch can enhance that little cove down there..." I advised, pointing out a small recess of sand sheltered between the craggy cliffs either side of it. "...Bringing it alive for the eye to behold."

"Crumbs! I'd never noticed that cove! I've walked past here dozens of times but..."

"You've probably been enjoying the greater view of the headland over there – which is understandable. Its beauty catches the eye."

"But how could I have missed that beautiful little cove?" Christina asked; bemused.

"Sometimes we can't see the wood for the trees! I'm an artist – it's my job to notice things, I guess."

Christina looked at me in earnest.

"You know..." She said after a few moments of deliberation. "You have hidden depths."

I was uncertain if to take this as a compliment or not. After all, did I appear so shallow at first glance?

"I have known you long enough to know that you are a 'thinker' but this is something different."

A thinker? 'Thinker' and I were rarely mentioned in the same sentence. Most people, including Jilly, had often ridiculed;

"That's your problem, Kat... You don't think!"

"Not so sure about that...I guess I'm a bit of a simpleton when it comes to thinking... Or so I'm told."

"Absolute rubbish!" Christina retorted stoutly. "Just because you don't prattle on about stuff like the rest of us, doesn't make your thoughts any the less significant. It's knowing what to do about them or how to voice them which makes the difference."

I wasn't entirely sure what Christina was getting at! Somehow, the person she was describing didn't seem to be me, but I was happy to accept the compliment.

I packed away my equipment and Christina packed away the picnic blanket and we turned for home. I glanced at my watch and was surprised to see that our adventure had taken us away from the hotel and our aunts for five hours! I imagined Aunt Phoebe's face as we re-entered the hotel, and my heart sunk.

"Leave your aunt to me." Christina beamed as if reading my mind.

"She'll be fizzing!" I frowned.

Christina slipped her arm through mine as we began to walk back.

"Your Aunt will be fine. As soon as we get back, go to your room; shower, change, whatever... You'll see..."

I wasn't as convinced as my companion! I had my doubts that Aunt Phoebe would ever trust me again! I knew my elderly relative – she would have expected us back within two hours. Her gold wrist-watch would have been well observed this day, with much mouth pursing, deep breaths, tuts and huffs!

The hot water cascaded over my head and bounced on my shoulders. I closed my eyes, enjoying the comforting effect the warmth had on my skin. I knew it wouldn't be long before my ears were assaulted by my Aunt's vicious tongue, so I took full advantage of my time alone in the shower. I had taken the precaution of locking my room door, in case Aunt Phoebe took it into her head to storm my chamber ranting and raving about being left to shift for herself. But time passed and no hammering at the door, or angry voices were heard in the corridor outside... Oh my God! Perhaps she'd been taken poorly; had a stroke or heart attack and at this very moment, fighting for her life in a hospital bed! What had I done? I'd been selfish putting myself first – going out, enjoying the company of a beautiful woman, who I knew I could never have, but I still had to do it! I jumped out of the shower and grabbed the towel. How would I explain this to Mum? I was supposed to be looking after Aunt Phoebe and now she was dead!

A light tap at the door made me start. I looked about the bedroom for an escape route. They had already arrived to point the finger of scorn at me! With wet hair and damp skin, I ran around the room like a lunatic, frantically picking up my discarded clothes and swearing when I caught my little toe on the bed-leg.

"Shit!"

"Kat! Are you ok?"

It was Christina's voice. I limped to the door and unlocked it.

"Hi." I said, breathlessly as I opened the door a little.

"Sorry to bother you. Is everything ok? I heard some strange noises coming from..."

"Yes... Sorry... Me! Running about like a loony!"

"You're wet!"

"Yes. Just got out of the shower." I replied, apologetically.

I pulled the towel about me tighter.

"Can I come in?"

"Err, yes... Of course."

I opened the door wider to allow my friend in.

"Sorry about the mess." I said, gesturing to the mounds of discarded clothes.

"Look! Forget that... I just wanted to warn you that your aunt is on her way up!"

"Oh bother!" I sighed. "I knew she'd blow her stack!"

"No... Not that... I'm afraid she's slightly unwell."

"I knew it! She's had a stroke, hasn't she? And it's all my fault!"

I broke out in a hot sweat and my heart thumped unmercifully. What was I going to tell Mum?

"No... It's not that... Oh Lord!"

"What's happened?" I asked, a little calmer.

Christina looked at me and started to giggle.

"What?" I asked bemused.

"I'm sorry, Kat... I shouldn't laugh... but... she's drunk!"

Chapter 9

"Drunk!" I shrieked in disbelief.

Christina nodded her head vigorously. She was beginning to turn red in the face as she tried to control her mirth.

"But how?"

When Christina had sufficiently composed herself, she took a paper tissue from her pocket and blew her moist nose.

"Oh dear, Kat! I'm so sorry, but you didn't witness what happened downstairs." She replied, still chuckling. "It appears that the two old ladies decided to have a little drink; the consequence of this is; they have polished off a full bottle of good sherry between them and are now pissed as farts!"

With this explanation, she exploded with laughter. I stood bemused. Was I really hearing this?

"Drunk? Aunt Phoebe? Pissed?"

Christina nodded, vigorously wiping the deluge of tears streaming down her face.

"Not only this…" She continued, "But they managed a half bottle of Port too!"

"So what did you witness downstairs?" I asked, anxiously.

"Dancing!" Christina spluttered.

I stood, I'm quite sure, opened-mouthed in disbelief, when the sound of what I can only describe as a cat howling, drew my attention. I ran to the bedroom door and popped my head out into the corridor. The sight which greeted me was certainly one to behold. Aunt Phoebe, propped up by two elderly gentlemen, staggered along the hallway. She had a strange, far-away look in her eyes; a look which I had never seen before.

"Aunt Phoebe!" I gasped, still clutching the hotel towel to my naked body. "What on earth have you been up to?"

"Ooh! Hello dear!" She responded in a very high-pitched, sing-song voice. "I've been having such a lovely time with Lucy."

"But who are these gentlemen?" I asked, glancing from one to the other.

"Albert and Henry. They have been looking after me... Haven't you?" She said, beaming at her associates.

"Don't worry... Albert and Henry are hotel regulars. They weren't involved in the drinking party which, according to Grace who was on duty this afternoon, has been going on since before luncheon!"

I stared at Christina who was still finding it hard to keep her composure.

"I really don't know what to say." I said, shaking my head.

"I do!" Aunt Phoebe, announced. "Let's have another glass of grog!"

"Grog?"

"Yes, dear... grog!" She slurred as she tottered up to me. And with very boozy breath, announced, "I know you keep a little bottle of something in your room, as I've seen it!" She proclaimed to the world.

"I don't keep booze in my room, Aunt!" I cried; quite offended.

"Albert! Come and have a snifter in my niece's room!" Aunt Phoebe boomed. "She doesn't mind in the slightest."

My Aunt took hold of the gentleman's hand and almost hauled him into my room. As he staggered by, one of his blazer buttons caught my towel. What happened next will haunt me forever! The button dragged the towel away from my body and followed him into the room like a bride's train.

"Oh my God!" Christina cried and flung herself at me.

I could feel her shaking with laughter as she attempted to protect my modesty. At any other time, this would have been a pleasure, especially with Christina, but I was in no mood for dallying with pretty girls, naked or otherwise.

"Please, Sir... Can you pass me my robe?" I pleaded with the other gentleman, whose eyes couldn't believe what they had just witnessed.

I pointed in the general direction of the bed and Henry darted by with his eyes averted. Aunt Phoebe and Albert were dancing around my boudoir to a tuneless rendition of something or another. Christina was choking with laughter.

"And where is your Aunt?" I asked incredulously.

"Passed out on the bar-room floor! I left Grace dealing with her. Oh Kat! You must see the funny side of this, surely?"

I felt too shocked to see the funny side of anything. Henry returned, holding out my robe with one hand and covering his eyes with the other. Poor man, he was so embarrassed. He looked a kindly old gent – the type who would always rise from his chair when a lady entered the room. Goodness knows what he made of my family at that moment.

I quickly unfastened myself from Christina's grip and rapidly enclosed the white robe around my body. I sighed – at least this was one problem solved. Christina, I noticed had entered my room with the intention of removing Albert from Aunt Phoebe's grip. I followed, and between us, managed to free the old gentleman. He was less shy than Henry and I do believe in retrospect, had probably enjoyed the experience, as his eyes were shining, gleefully.

"I'm so sorry." I muttered apologetically. "You must excuse my Aunt. She's a little... unwell at present."

"Blotto, more like! You should have seen what your relative and Mrs. King were guzzling in the bar. Quite a pair!" He chuckled mischievously. "Livened up this dreary, old dump, no end!"

He turned and left the room, joining his friend in the corridor.

"Kat!" Christina yelled.

I looked in her direction and beheld, to my shame, Aunt Phoebe; passed out in Christina's arms and slobbering over her shoulder like a drooling Labrador.

"Aunt Phoebe!" I groaned.

How would I ever live this down?

Chapter 10

Phoebe was now snoring happily in my bed. I observed her from the wicker chair in the corner of the room. I was still bemused by the whole spectacle. Had I really witnessed her, prancing around the corridors of this old fashioned hotel, drunk as a skunk and flirting with gentleman whom she had picked-up in the bar downstairs? Who would believe such a story? I'm sure neither my mother or sister would – at least not without some sort of photographic evidence and this, I did not have. A light tap at the door intruded upon my thoughts.

"Hi." Christina smiled, as she stood before me. "I thought you might want to pop downstairs and have some dinner."

I looked back at my Aunt and frowned.

"Perhaps later. I really need to keep an eye on my relative; just to make sure she's okay." I sighed.

"That's what I'm here for. I'll keep an eye – you eat your dinner. She'll be fine."

"What about your aunt? Who's keeping an eye on her?"

"Up and about and just polishing-off a sizable portion of fish pie!" She replied with a grin. "So, hop to it."

"I'm so sorry about Phoebe." I said, glancing at the elderly lady who snorted loudly. "I've never known her do anything like this before!"

"Kat... There's no need to apologise. I think we can split the blame between the pair of them. Besides, it's good to see that they can still let their hair down."

"I don't think I have ever seen Aunt Phoebe letting her hair down in my life!"

"It proves she's human."

I nodded.

"Go on... Go get something to eat before the dining room closes. Then, later, when it's a bit quieter... perhaps a drink?"

I glanced once more at the old lady and nodded in agreement. Christina took my hand and squeezed it affectionately. Her hand was warm and soft... Oh, so soft! I felt fluttering from deep within as she smiled at me. I imagined the taste of her lips and how they would feel pressed against my own, moving gently to begin with and then, becoming more passionate as the kiss deepened. Oh! How I needed that kiss and... and...

"Well..." She whispered, breaking into my erotic thought. "I've brought my book, so I'll see you a little later."

"Y-yes..." I stammered. "See you later."

Every pulse in my body was throbbing in want of this woman – a woman I knew I could never have. I hadn't felt this way about anyone in ages... not even Jilly - and amazingly, I hadn't realised. Jilly had been my world for so long that I never imagined I could feel such attraction to another soul. Maybe I was just home sick; I missed having a body close to mine at night... but then, Jilly often hugged the other side of our bed or would even sleep in the spare room.

"Kat." She'd say. "I can't sleep, so I'm going into the other room. I don't want to keep disturbing you."

"You're not." I would point out, rubbing my sleepy eyes.

"No, I've made my mind up. I'll see you at breakfast."

And off she'd trot... In retrospect, this had been happening more and more recently. I'd suggested that she might need to see a doctor but she just laughed it off. It was all to do with work; too much stress and worry keeping her awake. I also suggested perhaps she needed to change her job – somewhere they might appreciate her more, but she scorned the idea.

"Are you out of your tiny mind?" She boomed. "After all the hard work I've done for that place and you casually suggest I just stroll away, leaving all those other little shits to pick up my bonus? Not fucking likely!"

"It was only a suggestion." I replied meekly.

"Well, if that's as good as it gets, Kat, you'd best keep your mouth shut!"

She can be hurtful at times, but I suppose people like me need to be bullied into common sense periodically... don't you think? I admit that I'm not always the sharpest knife in the drawer and often lack concentration, but Jilly talks fast, frequently about work-related issues which I seldom understand. Once or twice I have asked her to explain, but she gets really irritated having to repeat herself.

"For God's sake, Kat, keep up!" She'd yell.

So, no visit to the doctor for sleeping advice and no change to her job. I wasn't sure what else I could do or say. So, instead, our erratic sleeping arrangements continued. It wasn't until I was toying with the last of my apple crumble that I realised how long this had been going on for. I was shocked to say the least. We had become so distant from each other that I couldn't even remember when she had last touched, or been intimate with me.

"Are you done with this, madam?" The waitress asked.

I was the last resident in the hotel dining room and clearly, she was anxious to get cleared away.

"Yes, thank you." I muttered, placing my napkin onto the table and rising to leave.

I found a heavy cloud of despair encroaching upon my world and felt uneasy. I wandered, unwittingly, to my bedroom deep in thought. Opening the door, I heard voices and one, in particular, which caught my attention.

"There you are dear." Aunt Phoebe, smiled, sitting up in bed as if nothing had happened. "Christina here has been looking after me, splendidly. I'm feeling a lot more like myself now, I'm pleased to say – there are so many viruses around these days – one has to look after one's self so carefully." She advised.

I glanced at Christina who raised her eyebrows.

"Well, I'm very pleased to hear you are feeling so much better, Aunt. Let's hope you don't have a relapse, later."

"Well, if I do, you'll be the first to know."

I did not doubt this!

"What I can't understand is, why am I not in my own room?"

Later, I left Aunt Phoebe tucked up warm and snug in my bed with an eau de cologne stick and a hot, non-alcoholic drink by her side. She complained bitterly of a headache, for which I administered pain killers. Christina had left the room upon my return and now, Auntie wanted a quiet night to herself and had banished me. I suspected she was in the early stages of a hangover and wanted to be left alone. Whether or not she actually remembered being drunk, I hadn't the slightest notion. So I left the room and wandered off down into the hotel lounge.

As I entered the room, I was met by several hard stares from some of the older residents of the hotel. Others were dozing in armchairs or watching a re-run of 'Last of The Summer Wine' but my presence in the room had caused a bit of a stir.

"If you want coffee; the waitress has finished for the evening!" I was informed by a little, bird-like woman sitting by the window. "No coffees served after eight o'clock. It will have to be tea! This is the rule of the hotel. Breakfast is from seven thirty until ten, and luncheon is served between twelve and two. Kindly do not smoke in the bedrooms or any other place in the hotel; a designated smoking area is available in the garden, to the rear of the building. Please ensure that all cigarette ends have been extinguished in the smoking-vessel provided."

I smiled uncomfortably. I wasn't sure if this monologue had been for my benefit or she was reciting a list of dos and don'ts from the hotel rule book as her 'party piece'. Therefore, I smiled sweetly and thanked her for her help. She seemed pleased and resumed her knitting. I glanced around the room and one or two of the spectators blinked and looked away, whilst others blatantly continued to gawp. A newspaper, lying folded on a coffee table, caught my eye and I stooped to pick it up. But before my fingers had a chance to grip it, a rather cutting voice spoke.

"That's Mr. Rushton's newspaper. He won't be pleased if anyone's touched it!"

I snatched my hand away like a naughty child and turned around. A small gentleman dressed in a perfectly fitted grey flannel suit stood almost touching my nose.

"You can't just take other people's things, you know."

"I-I wasn't going to steal it!" I confessed. "I just wanted to have a read before..."

"Now, now Mr. Lewis! Leave the lady alone. She isn't going to take anything away."

To my relief, Christina had entered the room with a tray of tea things.

"Now sit down there, and I'll pour your tea."

Mr. Lewis sat down but kept a beady eye on me. One or two oldies rose from their seats to receive a cup and saucer from Christina.

"Where are the biscuits, dear? I must have a biscuit with my tea! I couldn't possibly drink it without!" A lady who had previously been watching television, asked anxiously.

"They are here, Joyce." Christina pointed to a gaily coloured biscuit barrel.

"Here... Let me." I volunteered, stooping to pick up the tin.

There was a momentary look of dread in the old lady's eye, but I smiled and held out the tin and she shyly took out a Custard Cream.

"Now... Has everyone got a cup of tea and a biscuit?" Christina asked.

The residents muttered in response as they resumed their seats.

I glanced around and noted that Aunt Phoebe's gentlemen friends were sitting together at the far end of the room. Albert, the dancer, gave me a saucy wink while Henry, the witness to my nakedness, blushed heavily.

"Well, that's that... How about a drink?"

"Love one." I said gratefully.

Mr. Lewis who was still giving me the 'evil eye' was beginning to irritate me. I really don't know what came over me, but I casually picked up Mr. Rushton's newspaper and in a flurry of protest, headed for the lounge door.

Chapter 11

We sipped our drinks in the hotel's elegant court yard. There were still one or two residents hanging about – some of the more youthful ones, but we managed to find a quiet space of our own and settled for what was left of the warm evening.

Slowly as night began to fall, small colourful solar lights started to glow, one by one, and the evening became a fairy land. I looked up into the clear sky and could smell the warm sweetness of summer as the heat of the day began to recede. What a time we'd had! Spending all those wonderful hours with Christina, then the drunken, comedy spectacular which had starred our two remarkable aunts. To top it all, I was beginning to realise my feelings towards Christina were, perhaps, rather predatory and I needed to back off, but the revelation that things between Jilly and I were not as they should be, made me long for comfort.

"Penny for them?" Christina murmured.

I smiled rather regretfully. It wasn't every day that so many chickens came home to roost, but just now, my coop seemed pretty crammed with just this. I took a deep breath.

"Oh! I don't know. We had such a perfect day but then Aunt Phoebe happened and then..."

I paused here.

"And then what?" My companion asked compassionately. "Your Aunt will be none the wiser; unless you tell her what happened and at the end of the day, there was no real harm done. Just two old ladies having one or two sherries too many – it's not the end of the world, you know!"

"No, it's not about that. In retrospect, that was really quite funny... No, I found out something – about myself, today."

"Really?" Christina asked, uncertainly.

I nodded. Too embarrassed to look into my friend's eyes.

"My relationship isn't working anymore. It's been breaking down for some while now – I just haven't wanted to face it, I guess."

"And you found this out today?" Christina frowned.

"Yes."

Christina was quiet for a while. Probably wondering what had made me face reality.

"Have you spoken to your partner this evening?" She asked, wearily.

"No. I just know that it won't survive."

"I'm so sorry, Kat. I wish there was something I could do or say to make it feel better, but I know too well that only time can heal."

"You know I'm with a woman, don't you?" I asked quickly.

Christina looked a little astonished at my sudden outburst.

"Well, you didn't say... but... I assumed."

"We've grown apart, you see." I went on. "She lives her life and I live mine. Mine's much quieter. Jilly is very out-going – a real party animal. I'm just boring."

"But you aren't, Kat!" Christina protested. "You're not a... 'party animal', granted, but you are a compassionate, funny and loving person and if this... Jilly can't see this, then, it's her loss! I would love to remain your friend." She added gently.

Tears bubbled to the surface of my eyes. I so wanted to be loved by Christina – she would fill my life with all the good things that it had lacked for so long – the things which Jilly had starved me of, such as warmth of love and tenderness. Christina gathered me into her arms and held me tight. I wanted to curl up into a little ball and live in the comfort of her pocket forever.

Oh dear! What a pickle to find myself in. I felt like one of those women who wear their heart on their sleeve for the entire world to see. Folks...

this just isn't me! I'm the happy-go-lucky one – the one that never gets down over anything - the one that everyone else comes to see when they have a problem. This will never do. Pull yourself together, Kat!

"I'm sorry!" I gasped; pulling away from Christina's arms. "I really don't know what came over me."

"Hey! There's nothing to be sorry about. You're upset. The break-up of a relationship is always painful – I should know; I've been through it once or twice." She replied, soothingly.

"I'm not really sure where I go from here." I said miserably. "Do I go home and say to Jilly, that I've had enough – let's call it a day?"

"It's a start."

I emptied my glass and stood. Our out-door companions had drifted back into the hotel some time previously, and I didn't want to keep Christina up late as she was to rise early for the breakfast shift.

"Well, I'm for bed. Thanks for listening to me, droning on."

"Kat." Christina said, rising. "I know we haven't known each other that long, but I just want to say to you that I already value you as a friend and I hope you feel the same about me? Which means, you can tell or ask me anything – if it helps."

This was, indeed, an infusion of comfort; injected straight into my heart. I couldn't speak at that moment as I could feel the tears welling again. I just nodded vigorously and was glad to accept Christina's offer of another hug. Of course, from here on, I must try to avoid embraces with her – I wasn't sure my heart could take the pressure.

We walked slowly back into the hotel, making our way up to Aunt Phoebe's room. Christina had a pass-key to allow me access – seeing that my relative had commandeered my quarters.

"Thank you." I whispered at the door. "I don't know what I would have done without you tonight."

"Oh, shush." She grinned. "Go on in. Have a good night's sleep. I'll see you at breakfast."

"Goodnight."

"Goodnight Kat." She replied softly.

Sleep didn't come easily that night – there were too many topics whizzing around in my head to allow me to fall into an easy slumber. I did consider phoning Jilly – perhaps just hearing her voice might make everything better and prove that our relationship was still strong. The problem is, when there is a seed of doubt, the mind has a way of cultivating the spores, nurturing them, harvesting and spitting out the evidence. Now, my head was presenting me with an even more damning testimony of how our relationship had malfunctioned and was offering good reason why it should be ended.

I have already admitted that I was strongly attracted to Christina and in truth; I didn't believe it was a mere crush. I found it easy being in her company. She made me laugh and opened my mind up to things which previously, I might have ignored. I discovered her simple, almost child-like, enthusiasm for life, refreshing and found myself being carried away with her; transported into a Narnia-like fantasy.

Jilly found me boring – I knew this without need of clarification – I knew by her lack of interest in me; of my work; of my family and friends. These days, she didn't know me – I was a stranger to her and in truth, she was to me. We had out-grown each other, veering off in different directions. I suppose I'd been the last to realise this or was it that I just didn't want to admit it to myself?

I started having doubts of Jilly's fidelity; she had cheated on me once before, earlier in our relationship – I had forgiven her as she swore that the other woman had done all the chasing.

She'd been a victim of (how did she put it?) 'overwhelming flattery'! Being besotted with Jilly, I chose to forgive and forget – well, until now, that is. The more I thought of it, the more irritated I became – I tossed and turned – the sheet going one way and the pillow going another. How dare she fob me off with such tosh! I should have asked questions and demanded answers – it's too late now, but what an idiot I'd been... or perhaps desperate?

Every year of our relationship I now scrutinised, picking up on events and peculiarities which had occurred along the way. I'd been such a clot. No wonder Jilly laughed at me. What a mug!

By five thirty, I felt like I'd done fourteen rounds with a prize fighter! My eyes were heavy and dry from lack of repose and spasmodic tears. My head ached from over thinking and my heart felt heavy. I sat on the side of the bed and looked out at the sea-view from the window. My Aunt had always requested this room and now I understood why. My room overlooked the car park, but this room, with its view of the sea and the early morning sun shining on it, was nothing short of spectacular! I walked over and opened the window as wide as it would go and took deep breaths of the cooler, morning air. I wondered momentarily what sort of night my hung-over Aunt may have experienced and smiled at the scene which yesterday, had left me bemused. My affection for my Aunt grew warmer from that moment. She was cantankerous and down-right irritating at times, but she revealed an unexpected, vulnerable side to her nature which I found endearing. She liked to have the control, alright, but over the remaining days of our holiday, I was determined to offer her something different from her dull, tedious, holiday routine. I wanted to show her the breath-taking views Christina had shown me and take her to dinner in exciting restaurants and ply her with fine wines. I wanted to loosen up her straight-laced values; scratch the surface; discover her past;

how she'd lived and who she'd loved - find out about the person within.

I closed my eyes for a brief moment. I'd spent the last six hours in dark despair and now I felt like a wet weekend in Herne Bay! But I'd learned a lot about myself and considered that now was the time to stop living in the shadow of others, especially Jilly, and take control of my own destiny.

Chapter 12

"How are you Auntie?" I whispered as I entered the room.

"I'm feeling much better, thank you dear. Christina brought me up this lovely breakfast on a tray about twenty minutes ago – such a kind thought and such a lovely girl. She does remind me of my friend Lottie – always thinking of other people."

I smiled. This act of kindness was such a 'Christina' thing to do.

"You are very lucky, Aunt. How did you sleep?"

"Well, judging by those dark circles under your eyes, I'd say a lot better than you, dear!"

"Yes, I didn't sleep much."

"Well, I don't know what kept you awake dear, but I'm sure a good, hearty breakfast will help to restore your glow. You always look so healthy

Katherine, unlike your poor sister; it's a shame to see you all dowdy, like this."

I smiled. My Aunt had never praised me before and though this was more of a back-handed compliment, I accepted it with good grace. Though I'm not sure what my sister would have thought!

"I'm sure you are right, Aunt. Well, if you will excuse me, I'll pop downstairs, have breakfast, and if you feel up to it, I'm going to take you for a nice drive today – I have some beautiful views to show you, and then, I thought we might have a nice lunch out. The weather is glorious and Christina has told me about a little restaurant that serves exquisite luncheons."

"Oh!" She looked up from her boiled egg in surprise. "That sounds extremely nice, dear. It will be lovely to go out and see something of the old place. I can't remember the last time I did this. Certainly not since my Thomas passed."

Aunt Phoebe and Uncle Thomas had always been devoted to each other. Mother always said that Thomas was hen-pecked, but I don't think he suffered much by it. He had been a lovely old gentleman – always so tidy and very dapper in dress – hair neatly trimmed and brogues always shining. He'd died when I was about ten, but I remember these things about him. He would slip my sister Anna and I a fifty pence piece each time we saw him, and would always whisper;

"Go spend it all on sweets!"

We liked Uncle Thomas, very much!

"That's a long time ago, Aunt Phoebe - it's high time you saw it all again. I'll meet you here in about three quarters of an hour." I said, waving to my relative. "See you presently."

I exchanged a few, brief words with Christina. I knew I looked like shit and my Aunt had verified this, but my friend only showed compassion in her eyes and wished me a pleasant day.

The small road was steep and spiralled as we travelled higher and higher into the heavens until at last we reached the summit.

The weather was proving to be on my side and the sun's rays bounced off the sea below us. I'd found a parking bay along the cliff top and helped my Aunt from the car.

"This is very beautiful, dear!" She enthused. "I have vague memories of Thomas and I having tea somewhere along here. Have you got my handbag, dear?"

"Yes, Aunt – it's here. Just look at that sea. Isn't it wonderful?"

Seagulls were swooping and plunging; crying out to each other as they frolicked in the clear blue sky. I love this sound – it always evokes holidays of old; good times before life became over complicated.

"You're very quiet, Katherine – you've hardly murmured since we left the hotel."

"Sorry… Just got a few things on my mind at the moment."

"You're far too young to be nursing concerns. You're not ill, are you?"

"No Aunt." I chuckled. "I'm quite healthy, but thank you for asking."

"It's not that young man in the hotel bothering you, is it dear? Has he asked you out to dinner? You mustn't be too nervous to accept, you know."

"No Aunt, and you know, he's not that young. I heard him say to one of the waitresses that he was sixty-two and chasing retirement!"

"Goodness! I thought he was only in his early fifties! Still, a good catch all the same."

I just smiled. It seemed to me that however many times I tried to explain my sexuality, it just went in one ear and gushed out the other! It was easier to allow her to ramble on.

We strolled along the cliff path until reaching a kiosk selling soft drinks and teas. I asked Aunt Phoebe if she would like a cup, but she screwed up her nose.

"Where is their fresh water supply, Katherine?" She replied in a big, loud voice. "They probably use sea water or worse! Speaking of which, I need to spend a penny, dear."

Oops! How was I going to handle this one?

"Err... I'm not sure where the nearest toilet is, Aunt. Can you hold it for a bit?"

"No dear!" She replied in an astonished voice.

"Ok... I'll just ask the proprietor of the tea place."

I left Aunt doing an inventory check in her hand bag. No doubt checking her supply of tissues, pain killers and Polo Mints.

"Excuse me..."

A rather slouchy looking young woman who had been washing up tea cups, looked up from her task.

"Can I 'elp?"

"Do you know where the nearest toilets are please? My Aunt is in need of one and..."

"None 'round 'ere, love!" She declared. "You'll 'ave to drive back down to the first car park you passed – they've got bogs there."

"Oh dear..."

"Or she can 'itch up her skirt and wee behind that gorse bush over there. It's the one I use."

"Right... Thank you." I replied, just imagining my Aunt's face if I suggested this!

"Aunt, I'm afraid we will have to go back to the car and drive to that first car park we passed. Apparently there's some toilets there."

Phoebe gazed at me in astonishment.

"No lavatories!" She cried. "Katherine! I'm not sure I can wait that long! It's my water tablets, you see... They start to work at eleven fifteen and there's no stopping me."

Why couldn't she have explained this before we left the hotel?

"Goodness me." I murmured.

The girl in the tea kiosk emerged and leaned against the little cabin smoking a cigarette and fiddling with her mobile phone. She looked up at us in amusement.

"Looks like it's the gorse bush or nothing!" She chuckled.

Chapter 13

"Please make sure that nobody is looking." Aunt Phoebe instructed as she squatted behind the gorse bush. "I've never felt so humiliated in my entire life!" She boomed.

I glanced up at the tea kiosk. The young girl serving had just stubbed out her cigarette and was now grinning inanely at us.

"Are you still holding my handbag, Katherine?"

"Yes, Aunt." I sighed.

"Then pass me over that packet of tissues in there and keep guard!"

I did as instructed and resumed my vigil at the gorse bush. Thankfully, most walkers passed by without glancing in our direction, but once or twice, I detected a look of genuine empathy from women who were laden with children and elderly parents. They had done this; they had been the look-out, the holder of items, and the passer of neatly folded scented tissues at the watering hole! They knew and they understood! I half-smiled by return, in recognition of their demonstration of solidarity.

"You'll have to help me up, Katherine." The elderly lady instructed.

I was there in a heartbeat, taking her arms and heaving her upright again. She fidgeted around for a few moments, ensuring that no sign of underwear was showing and that all evidence of those few, shameful moments had been eradicated for ever. She emerged from the undergrowth like Boudicca, ready for battle and prepared to challenge anyone who may have shown the slightest amusement. The young woman from the tea kiosk watched our proceedings with great interest before her attention was diverted by an interesting post on Facebook.

We walked slowly back to the car. Our morning of sight-seeing abandoned in favour of returning to the hotel until my Aunt's present bladder problem had quietened. I helped her in and we set off.

After a moment or two, I became aware of a slight odour in the car. I wrinkled my nose but continued without comment. My Aunt became fidgety, looking about her crossly before crying;

"Really, Katherine! It just isn't becoming of a woman of your age! Kindly control yourself and open a window!"

I gasped in horror at the accusation which had just been hurled at me.

"It wasn't me, Aunt, I promise you!" I protested as I negotiated the sharp bends on our descent.

"Well, it certainly wasn't me!"

The smell grew stronger as she shuffled about indignantly and then I saw it. Smeared on the sole of her peep-toe sandals was a very smelly lump of dog's poo! She must have trodden in it as she emerged from the watering hole and in a bid to get comfortable in the car, had rubbed it nicely around the passenger car mat. I sighed. What a mess!

"Oh dear, Aunt. I think you've trodden in something nasty!" I advised.

"What!" She shrieked.

I pointed to her sandal. She looked down and huffed.

"Why didn't you point this out to me earlier?" She yelled. "Really Katherine! You are supposed to be helping me, this holiday. So far, I've seen little evidence of it!"

So now it was my fault! My fault that she takes water tablets and has to pee at the drop of a hat, my fault that there was no provision of toilet facilities up on top of a cliff and my fault that she had walked in dog's shit and smothered it all over my car mats. Gee-whiz!

"You should be grateful that I bring you along with me and how do you repay me...?" She continued unabashed.

"I think that's quite enough, Aunt!" I replied, firmly.

She turned to me, indignantly.

"How dare you speak to me in that tone?"

I pulled to the side of the narrow road and stopped the car.

"Aunt!" I boomed. "If you can't behave, I will be taking you home – not to the hotel, but back to Sevenoaks! I will not have this behaviour in my car!"

She was silent. My little outburst had rocked her and she was speechless! I started the car and moved on.

We arrived back at the hotel twenty minutes later – twenty silent minutes later. I helped Aunt out of the car and instructed her to remove her sandal. I think she was about to protest when she looked at my face and decided to obey.

I ushered her into the hotel – what a funny sight we must have looked – Aunt Phoebe limping; wearing only one sandal, being escorted by a tight-lipped niece carrying, at arm's length, the other rather dubious shoe. Christina looked up from the reception desk and opened her mouth to speak. She took one look at my face and remained silent. My Aunt left me to seek the nearest toilet and I turned to Christina and grimaced.

"Oh dear God! What happened?" She squealed.

"It's a long story – what can I do with this?" I asked, waving the offending sandal in the air.

Christina's face contorted in horror.

"This way. Quick!"

She guided me through to a little area with a lean-to at the back of the hotel. It was used to store various garden tools and buckets. To the side, there was an outside tap over a drain which the gardener attached a long hose to, for watering the garden and court yard.

"Here! Give me that... I'll wash it off for you." Christina volunteered, holding out her hand.

"No! I'll do it." I replied.

"Kat... Go and see to your aunt. I'll sort this one out. Then, I'll organise some tea and when your aunt has settled, you can tell me what happened."

I sighed my gratitude and sped off in search of the old lady. I found her waiting for the lift and looking rather sheepish.

"Come on Auntie. Let's get you back to your room to tidy up and then Christina is going to organise some tea for us." I said as kindly as I could.

"It's all very well for you, Katherine. I'm old! I can't keep up like I used to."

I wasn't entirely sure I understood where my Aunt was coming from at that moment, but I made all the right noises in all the right places and by the time we reached her bedroom, she had calmed down.

"Thank you, dear." She said as I was about to leave her room. "I'll see myself downstairs shortly. There's no need to wait."

I closed the door behind me and felt awful. I'd been unnecessarily unkind to my Aunt – she hadn't purposely trodden in poo just to wind me up. I could have been a little more understanding. When I got downstairs, Christina was laying out some cups and saucers and a variety of biscuits for us. Phoebe's sandal was scrubbed clean and was drying off behind the reception desk. I thanked my friend and described our morning adventure. Christina laughed and laughed.

"Poor Kat!" She said in between bursts of mirth. "Don't worry about your car mat. We can sponge that off easily enough. There's some stuff the cleaner uses for just such occasions."

I nibbled on a biscuit which Christina had offered me.

"There's no need to feel guilty about how you handled it, Kat. Your Aunt is a very strong minded woman and will walk all over you if you let her. It doesn't harm, occasionally, to let her know that you are not actually a child anymore."

"She looked so helpless, just now." I wailed.

"She'll live to tell the tale, don't you worry. She'll probably dine out on it for months!"

I wasn't so sure about that, but Christina was right. Aunt Phoebe, like most other people, had habitually walked all over me for years and now it must stop.

Aunt Phoebe appeared at the lift doors, refreshed and ready for a nice cup of tea. Christina's Aunt Lucy waved to her from the lounge and the two old ladies became deep in conversation within moments. I hung around the reception area; just to be with Christina. She faffed around with paperwork and answered several telephone enquires as I sipped my tea. After a while, she straightened her paperwork and clipped the sheets together with a peg.

"There." She said. "Finished. At least Poppy can take over now. How are you feeling?"

"Much better, thanks."

"It's amazing what a nice cup of tea can do."

I wasn't so sure it was the tea which had worked magic – I believed it was the company.

"Look here... It's getting on for twelve thirty; our two aunts seem to enjoy each other's company pretty well, so why don't we collect them up, throw them into my car and take them out for a nice lunch. We can go to the place I recommended; Martin, the guy who owns it is a personal friend of mine. I'll give him a ring and I'm sure he'll find a table for us somewhere. What do you say? Are you game?"

"Of course, but don't you have other things you need to do? You've spent so much time on us already."

"The hotel owes me plenty of time and we have a full staff in today, so I can escape with a clear conscience. I'll phone Martin and you seek out the aunties to see what they say."

Before long, we were sitting on the veranda of a very, trendy bistro overlooking the sea. Martin had recommended and was preparing our lunches as we sipped on chilled white wine. The old ladies were sitting on the shadier side of the terrace while Christina and I donned sunglasses and relaxed in the early afternoon sun.

"Gosh! This is the life." I murmured.

"Mmm. Such a treat. You haven't said anymore about last night." Christina remarked suddenly.

"No. I spent most of the night thinking and planning and though I lost most of my sleep, at least I know where I'm going now."

"And where might that be?"

"As soon as I get back home, I'm going to leave Jilly. I'm starting afresh. I'm going to live my own life from now on."

"Bravo!" Christina cheered.

"What was that, dear?" Aunt Lucy asked, looking over the top of her spectacles.

"Kat has decided to move house, Auntie. Start a-fresh somewhere else." She declared, grinning at me.

"And what does your lady friend think of this?" Aunt Lucy asked me without ceremony.

I was tongue-tied; shocked that she even knew my circumstances.

"It's such a shame when relationships break down, don't you think, Phoebe? But it seems to be the way of the world these days." She declared sadly.

"What are you talking about, dear? Katherine isn't in one! I'm forever trying to find decent suitors for her, like Mr. Jenson back at the hotel, but she just won't have any of it." Aunt Phoebe advised.

"What Herbert? He's a ponce dear..."

I spluttered over these words.

"...He is at the hotel every season, scrounging and trying to seduce women to get money out of them. Isn't that right, Christina?"

"Aunt... I can't say such things about our hotel guests!"

"I can and I will! You know I'm right."

Christina shot me a look. My lips twitched into a smile.

"And, Phoebe dear, your niece won't be interested in the likes of Herbert Jenson, after all... he is a man. She requires quite a different frontal arrangement!"

A deadly silence hung over our table. I glanced tentatively at my Aunt for a reaction. She blinked a couple of times as she processed this bulletin from her friend. After a few moments, she cleared her throat.

"I beg your pardon, Lucy?"

Lucy tutted and took a deep breath.

"Your niece wants a woman, dear, not a man!"

"What on earth does she need a woman for, Lucy? You're talking absolute drivel."

"Aunt Lucy... I really don't think we should be discussing Kat's love life like this... After all, it's her business." Christina said with a blush.

"Nonsense dear! Best all out in the open, I think. Too much old stodge with us oldies... Time we faced facts and live and let live!"

I was learning that Aunt Lucy was quite a progressive old girl.

"Most men aren't fit for anything much, let alone satisfying a woman. They act and talk big but at the end of the day, they are only in it for their own satisfaction."

I glanced again at my Aunt. Her face was a picture of astonishment.

"Well, I must say, I didn't expect to hear such things coming from your lips, Lucy King. You certainly have surprised me!"

Aunt Phoebe shuffled around in her chair and looked slightly embarrassed.

Christina's friend, Martin, broke the silence as he walked out with a tray of freshly dressed crab and salad.

"Gosh! This looks wonderful!" I found myself saying in a great, loud voice.

Chapter 14

Martin served our lunch and after a brief chat involving mainly Christina and her aunt, left the veranda. I dug straight into my portion and wished the afternoon over as quickly as possible. Christina, bless her, managed to turn the topic of conversation away from my love life and onto something more appropriate for luncheon – her Aunt's bunion! Like many old folks, Aunt Lucy was in her element whilst discussing health issues and gave her niece chapter and verse as to why the doctor would not countenance a small, surgical procedure. I noticed that my Aunt remained unusually silent and hardly touched her dressed crab – even though it was a favourite. I felt duty bound to ask if she was quite well.

"I'm well enough, Katherine." She replied, icily.

I glanced at Christina who had managed, at long last, to hush her aunt.

"Is there something wrong with your lunch, Mrs. Hawkins?" She asked politely.

"Katherine! This will not do!" Auntie exploded. "How can you bring such shame upon your family?"

"I'm sorry Aunt, but I don't know what you're talking about." I lied.

"Sleeping with women!"

I felt our companions tense and shift uncomfortably. In fact, the whole resort became silent as Phoebe's words ricocheted around the small town, out to sea, hitting the boom and recoiling back to hit me in the ear.

After a brief moment, Aunt Lucy opened her mouth to speak but Christina hurriedly put a sock in it.

"Aunt Phoebe, no one is bringing shame on our family. I've been gay all my life – everyone knows and accepts it... all except you. Mother has explained it to you and so has Anna, many times, but you never listen."

My Aunt appeared quite shaken. I do believe to this very day that she was completely shocked by this revelation. Her face went quite grey and I wondered if she might be having heart failure.

"Phoebe dear, you must accept that times are different – we are not all the same and a jolly good job we're not!" Lucy reminded her, kindly. "You and I... well, we've had our time and husbands – lived our lives as we wanted, and with whom we wanted – now let the young folks do the same. I'm sure the world would be a better place if we just learned to accept everyone for what they are."

"That's all very well for you to say, Lucy, but you don't understand!" My Aunt explained, getting more agitated. "If she doesn't have a child, whom shall I leave my property to?"

I looked around sharply.

"What do you mean? Property?"

My Aunt took a scented tissue from her hand bag and wiped her nose.

"I've never told you this, Katherine, but when I'm dead and gone, you may inherit my entire estate... lock, stock and barrel."

"But you only have your little home in Sevenoaks!" I pointed out. "And I thought you'd bequeathed that to mum."

"That's quite right dear, I have... But you see, I have also a home in Scotland, Wales and Ireland. They were left to me by... Well, should I have been able to keep a child instead of having miscarriages, I would naturally have passed the property down through the Hawkins family line, but ..."

"You had miscarriages?" I cried incredulously. "I never knew..."

"I'm a private person, Katherine – I rarely talk about it."

"But all the same... Why did Mum never say anything?"

"She had her reasons."

I blinked in wonder.

"But how does this affect Katherine?" Christina enquired.

The old lady studied her crab salad for a few moments before raising her head again.

"Because Katherine is my illegitimate child."

"What?" I cried.

"Sorry... Can you repeat that?" Christina gasped, glancing at me.

Aunt Lucy's mouth opened in shock and her top-plate dropped from its resting place.

"Yes, Katherine dear... It's quite true."

How I didn't faint away completely, I'll never know. I certainly felt myself going. I think Christina may have pushed my head between my knees and splashed cold water on my face. I can remember seeing spots before my eyes and hearing my heart beating very loudly, but little else. I was speechless. I had not seen this one coming, at all! It had never occurred to me that I was the child of anyone other than Mum and Dad and now, I was totally devastated.

"No! No! No!" I cried. "My Mum is my Mum... Not you!"

I jumped up from the table and leant over the balustrade overlooking the narrow cobbled road which lead down to the sea front. I took deep breaths, hoping that I was just having a nightmare... I told myself I would wake shortly and everything would be alright.

"But I thought you couldn't have children. Didn't you just say that you'd had miscarriages?" Christina asked incredulously.

"Yes, but that was with my husband, Thomas."

"And Katherine?" Aunt Lucy enquired carefully. "Who was the father?"

So, not only do I start to learn that my parents aren't my parents, but I'm illegitimate too!

Aunt Phoebe turned to face me.

"Some years ago, I'm afraid I was a little indiscreet with a man who was a business associate of your Uncle Thomas. He worked in

Hong Kong when it was still British, but several times a year, Gordon – that was his name, came back to London for quarterly meetings and always stayed with Thomas and I. Obviously, we got to know Gordon quite well and we looked forward to his visits. Well, it so happened that, one evening, we had three tickets to the opera, but Thomas fell ill. Now, instead of abandoning our plans, Thomas insisted that we, Gordon and I, should continue and go. At first we opposed this, but Thomas could be persuasive, even when ill. So Gordon and I set off for London. We were eating first; Gordon suggested dining at his club in St. James's."

"Oh! How lovely." Aunt Lucy enthused. "I'm sure you had a wonderful meal."

Christina shot her aunt a warning look.

"Yes, it was dear – very pleasant indeed. I'll always remember that meal – it was chicken, but cooked in the most exquisite sauce. I asked the chef for the recipe and have cooked it on numerous occasions since."

"And what was the opera, dear?"

"Err, Aunt Lucy... Perhaps you should let Mrs. Hawkins continue with her story." Christina suggested kindly.

She looked at me with such compassion that it broke my already, fractured heart.

"Well..." Aunt Phoebe continued. "We had a wonderful evening – wine, wonderful food, music and the best company. We laughed and laughed and somehow, I forgot all about my poor Thomas at home. Anyway, the following night, we went to the theatre followed by a meal at a very swanky Soho restaurant, and after, he took me to a night club. It was all so daring but somehow, I couldn't resist the attraction of it all... and of him!"

I listened without comment. Was all this true or was it all part of a weird fantasy which my Aunt was having? She was so much older than my mother that I could hardly believe she would have conceived a child at all. She must have been at least forty-eight when she had me. How was I going to cope with this? I hated the thought of my life moving sideways. Nothing was constant anymore – not Jilly nor my family, it seemed. I was lost to them all. I was a lost soul out on a rough ocean. Where would it all end?

Chapter 15

"... So, you had an affair with him?" Aunt Lucy asked impertinently.

"Well, yes... I suppose I did."

"Gracious Heavens!" I yelled. "Of course you had a fucking affair with him! How the hell do you explain me, otherwise?"

Christina touched my arm gently as if trying to calm me. Calm me? Huh! I felt anything but calm at that moment. I felt sick.

"Katherine! Kindly watch your language. Besides... Your uncle never knew."

"You have the audacity to tell me to watch my language when you've lied to me all these years! And you even lied to Uncle Thomas!" I cried.

"I think perhaps we all need to calm down." Christina suggested. "Look, I'll ask Martin if you can have the use of his back room. It will be a private place for you both to speak without the whole town butting in."

I nodded my agreement. Within a few minutes, my Aunt and I entered a charming little room which also overlooked the bay.

"Can I get you any coffees?" Martin asked, kindly.

"I would like a nice cup of tea, please, if it's not too much trouble." My Aunt requested.

"Certainly." Martin answered with a smile.

"I'll have tea as well, please." Aunt Lucy chimed in.

"No, Aunt Lucy! Let Katherine and her aunt discuss their business in private. We'll have our tea on the terrace."

"But dear...!"

"No buts... Come on. Walk!"

Poor Aunt Lucy! She was so disappointed. At any other time, I would have been delighted with the situation, but as I was featured as the centre of this travesty, I couldn't really see the funny side of it.

Christina frog-marched her aunt away from the room leaving Phoebe and I alone. Martin arrived shortly afterwards with coffee and tea which was a blessing as the silence between my relative and I was deafening! He left the room giving me a comforting wink. I took up my coffee mug and sipped the scalding liquid by way of something to do, but regretted it afterwards. I heard my Aunt take a deep breath.

"Well, we can't undo what is done, Katherine." She announced profoundly.

"You mean; you don't want to! I'm not quite sure where I figure here."

"Nothing has changed, dear. You are still Stephanie's daughter – just not her biological one. I'm still your aunt and that's all that can be said."

"It's that simple for you, isn't it?"

"Well, yes…"

I shook my head sadly.

"Well, I wish it were for me."

"Look, Katherine... I never wanted a child by anyone other than my husband – it was pure fluke that I fell with Gordon's child! What do you want me to say? That I'm sorry?"

"It might be a start."

"Don't be so childish!" She hissed.

"Aunt Phoebe! Look, you had a child – a child which wasn't your husband's and you casually ignore the fact that he didn't even know it was his?"

"He didn't know it was his child because he didn't know I was pregnant."

"What?"

"When I found out, I knew immediately that it wasn't Thomas's child. We hadn't made love for months and... well, to begin with, I expected to lose the baby. But week by week, the child was still in me and I got past the first three months and apart from the appalling morning sickness, all was well."

"Except Uncle Thomas didn't know!"

"No, he didn't. The biggest secret I had ever kept from him – bless him." Aunt Phoebe murmured sadly.

"How did you get away with it?"

"I went away. He had seen my sickness in the mornings, but like an innocent lamb, he had no idea I was pregnant – after all, we'd not had sex for many months as he hadn't felt up to it. It appears his illness had started and... Well, you know his history. He had no reason to believe that I'd slept with another man, and therefore, just assumed that I was poorly. So, he suggested that I went abroad for a few months to get some sun. It was the perfect solution. So, I left, but I had to confide in someone – that someone was your mother. She was newly married to your father, but he, being in the army, was often from home, so I offered my child to her."

"What? How could you do such a thing? And how did you get away with it?" I asked incredulously.

"I asked her to pretend it was her child."

I sat, opened mouthed, trying to understand what I was hearing. My Aunt had fallen for another man's child and had casually palmed it off on her younger, newly married sister!

"Despicable! So not only did you lie to your husband, but you got my mother to lie to my father!"

"He may not have taken you on if he'd known the truth!" She argued. "So your mother pretended she'd fallen pregnant during their honeymoon."

"Dear God!"

Suddenly, movement at the bow window caught my eye. First it was a hand, then an arm and then, Aunt Lucy's face! She was trying to get as close to the open window as possible, probably to listen to our conversation. She had no idea I had seen her and I watched, fascinated, as she focused on her mission. Her mouth was slightly open and the point of her tongue touched her upper lip in concentration. I had an awful need to laugh! As tragic as things were, I had to laugh and laugh and laugh!

Chapter 16

By the time Christina had found her sleuthing aunt, I was completely senseless on the floor. My aunt was beginning to panic and calling out for help. As hard as I tried, I couldn't stop laughing. Tears rolled down my cheeks and my nose ran uncontrollably. Christina, with her Auntie in hot pursuit, rushed into the room and fell on her knees, by my side.

"What happened?" She cried, looking up at my relative anxiously.

"I just don't know. One moment she looked like she was about to kill me and in the next, she just started to laugh – she's got worse and worse and now I don't know what to do with her!"

"Kat! Kat!" Christina cried, shaking me by the shoulders. "Kat! Come on... Stop laughing!"

The next thing I felt was a stinging blow across my left cheek. I immediately stopped laughing and held my breath. I looked up into Christina's concerned eyes and promptly burst into tears. She took hold of me and pulled me close; hugging me tightly.

"It's ok... It's ok... She repeated over and over. Somehow, at that moment, I knew everything would be ok but there would be a lot of sludge to trudge through before my life was normal again... If ever.

Later, back at the hotel, after a hot bath and forty winks, I emerged from my room and sought out Christina. I found her busy sorting menus for the evening meal.

"How are you feeling, Kat?" She asked sympathetically.

"Well, I've had better days."

"How did you leave things with your aunt?"

I pulled a face.

"Well, I found out that after making the biggest mistake of her life, she managed to connive her way out of it and came up smelling of violets!"

"We all make mistakes, Kat." Christina pointed out compassionately.

"I know, but she's always been such an exacting person – always scornful of other people's weaknesses and rarely forgiving."

"How did it all happen, if you don't mind me asking?" Christina enquired, apologetically.

I told Christina the whole story and from time to time, her eyebrows rose in amazement.

"Gosh!"

"Gosh indeed. My poor Mum – my poor Dad!" I corrected, quickly.

"I wonder if he knows, after all this time."

"Well, if he does, he's never said anything." I replied.

Christina looked thoughtful for a few moments and then frowned.

"But this still hasn't explained why you need to have a child, Kat?"

This was a good point! And with all the drama of lunch time, it hadn't been fully explained. It was as if a vital piece of the jigsaw puzzle was missing.

"I will have to speak to my aunt again, as much as I don't want to."

I took myself off for a long, solitary walk. I believed time alone would do me good – bring some perspective to my unhappy situation. But before long, I felt the need of a mother's comfort and telephoned home.

"Hi love!" She answered cheerfully. "How's it going with Phoebe?"

I took a deep breath before answering.

"Oh well, you know Phoebe – she has her moments." I muttered.

"It won't be for too much longer, love." Mum commiserated. "Just a few more days then, you'll be rid of her."

This was true, but now I had received the added bonus of horrendous tidings about myself which in truth, I'd have preferred not to know.

"What's your weather been like?" She continued. "It's been glorious here. Your dad keeps moaning about having to water the garden every night and the grass is growing like the clappers!"

I chuckled. I could imagine him complaining.

"Have you heard from Jilly?"

"No. I spoke to her the other evening, but she cut short the call as she was going out."

Mother huffed.

"Couldn't she have gone out ten minutes later? I suppose we should be grateful that she condescended to return from her weekend away in Dublin?"

I could hear the sarcasm in Mum's voice. She didn't like Jilly very much. Never had really. I think she just tolerated her for my sake.

"Well, I guess she had her reasons for going out."

"Kat... Are you ok sweetheart? You sound a bit low!"

I couldn't stop the unexpected flow of tears which suddenly cascaded from my eyes. I so wanted to be with my mum at that moment – the mother who had been with me all my life, made sacrifices for me, bathed my grazed knees, taught me long division, cuddled me on the sofa during sad films and listened to my every moan and groan. The mother who had told me everything would be alright when I confessed to preferring girls to boys – the mother who I knew would defend me until her dying breath.

"Kat, what's wrong, love?"

"I'm sorry..." I sobbed uncontrollably. "I'm so sorry..."

"Kat! What's happened? For heaven's sake, love... talk to me!"

"Oh, Mum... I don't know what to say. I need to talk to you, but I can't over the phone!" I wailed.

"It's something to do with Jilly, isn't it?" She ranted. "She's dumped you, hasn't she? I just knew it... The little vixen! I'd like to give her a piece of my mind! I've never liked, her, Kat and I knew it would all end in tears. Always thinks she's better than everyone else...!" She continued.

"Mum!" I cried. "Stop, please! It's nothing to do with Jilly... Well, it's a bit to do with her, but mostly it's to do with me."

"What's wrong? Are you ok? Perhaps you should see a doctor if you aren't well?" She suggested fearfully.

Sometimes, mums go off on a tangent, predicting what you might be trying to tell them, which can be mildly irritating especially when they are barking up the wrong tree!

"Health wise, I'm fine, honestly. Please don't worry."

My tears paused for a while and I wiped my wet face with a tissue and perched on the promenade wall, looking out to sea.

There was silence at the other end of the phone. I wasn't sure how to broach the subject of my birth, so took advantage of this silence to try and find an opening line.

"It's Phoebe, isn't it?" Mum asked apprehensively. "She's dead, isn't she?"

"No, mum!" I laughed. "No, Aunt Phoebe is alive and kicking."

I could have added 'more's the pity' but somehow, this didn't seem appropriate.

"Then, what?"

"Mum... She's told me..."

"Told you what?"

"She's told me about... my birth."

There was another long silence at the other end. It only then occurred to me what a deep impact this might have on Mum – what sort of crisis it could start, especially as I assumed, Dad still didn't know the truth.

"Oh... Kat." Mum spoke at last. "I don't know what to say! Why the hell did she tell you?" I could feel her anger rising with each word she spoke. "It was my place to tell you, if anyone. You are my daughter! It was up to me if you should know or not!"

There was a sob in her last few words. She was devastated and I had been the cause of it. Why had I felt it necessary to contact her? Simply because she was my mum. And now she was upset and crying, and it was all my fault.

"Mum! Please don't cry... It's alright!"

"But I've let you down!" She wailed.

"No you haven't! I'm fine about it. I was shocked at first, but it makes no difference to me. I still love you... but even more now! Please don't get upset about it. Dad will wonder what's happened and..."

"Your dad doesn't know... please don't..."

"I know, Mum. I would never breathe a word to him."

"He'd never forgive me if he knew! It would break his heart. You know you are his favourite!"

"But he's not going to know, Mum! It's our secret. As much as I don't like secrets, I fully understand why you have never said anything to him. I don't want him to know, or Anna, either."

"But why did Phoebe tell you?"

"We were trying to explain to her why I don't want to be with a man and..."

"We?"

"I've made a friend at the hotel, Mum. Her name's Christina. She has an aunt too, and this all started while we were having lunch together, today and..."

"Look Kat... I'm going around in circles here. I think the best thing I can do is to motor down – then, we can talk. I'll come down tomorrow morning – I'll be there for about lunch time."

"What about Dad?"

"I'll just tell him that Phoebe is unwell and I want to check on her."

"I'm sorry, Mum." I said, still feeling guilty.

"You've got nothing to be sorry for, love. In a funny way, I'm glad you know. It's just come as a bit of a shock."

"Yeah, for us both. I love you, Mum – you know that, don't you?"

"Yes love, I do. I love you too, darling. See you tomorrow."

Chapter 17

Aunt Phoebe was having dinner in her room; probably the best thing under the circumstances. I still felt too emotional to broach the subject of children and therefore, ate alone. I felt every eye on me as I entered the dining room – as if every resident was aware of my new situation and judging me. This, of course, was utterly ridiculous and I'm sure it was mere curiosity which made them eye me. Most residents were elderly apart from one or two young families. It was one such family which drew back the attention of the older folks when a little girl threw her plate of fish fingers and mashed potatoes over her brother. This resulted in screams of indignation and tantrums. I ignored the mayhem and concentrated on the evening's menu.

"Can I take your order, please?"

I looked up. Maria, the waitress stood before me expectantly, with notebook and pen poised.

"Err… Soup… Salmon and the Lemon Mousse to follow, please."

She thanked me for my order and bustled away.

"Excuse me, dear…"

I looked over my shoulder. A small, wizened lady, probably in her late eighties grinned at me with over-sized false teeth.

"I wonder if I can bother you, dear."

"Of course." I replied, rising from my seat. "How can I help?"

"Well…" She replied, confidentially. "I've been rather a silly, old woman and dropped my hearing aid on the floor somewhere. My eyes aren't too good these days and I can't find the blessed thing!"

She lifted the damask table cloth and peeked beneath.

"Of course." I smiled. "Here… Let me."

I got onto my hands and knees and went under the table. The elderly lady held up the table cloth to let in some light as I fumbled around on the dark floor for her gadget.

"I'm so sorry to be such a nuisance, my dear. I'm a bit of a nuisance to everyone these days. That's one of the joys of getting old, I'm afraid."

"Please don't worry." I smiled as I rose with a strange object between my fingers. "Is this it?"

My experience with hearing aids had been limited.

"Oh! Thank you!" She beamed. "I am so obliged to you. You've been so kind."

"It was a pleasure."

"It's my first night here…" She confided. "And I'm a little nervous. And when I'm nervous, I shake a little. I'm such a silly, old thing."

"I'm sure you will settle in soon. It's a lovely hotel and they will look after you."

"I'm sure they will. You see, I lost my husband earlier this year – we always did everything together, but since then, I've felt quite out on a limb. My niece suggested I should have a little holiday and arranged this for me, but I think I might have been happier staying at home."

I smiled.

"I'm sure she meant well."

"Oh yes! Indeed. She's very kind. But... Oh, well..." She replied, shrugging it off resolutely.

"I'm sure you'll be fine."

"Yes, of course. Thank you dear."

I smiled again and returned to my seat. I heard the waitress taking the elderly lady's order.

"... Thank you dear. You've been so kind." She said as the waitress walked away.

I turned around.

"Would you like some company at your table?" I asked.

I felt sorry for the old lady. She was not a demanding, troublesome old thing like Aunt Phoebe, but lonely and out of her comfort zone – the least I could do was to offer.

"Oh! That is so kind of you! Yes, please join me. Perhaps the waitress will lay an extra place if we call her back."

"It's alright... I'll just bring my knife and fork over with me. It will save her the trouble."

The old lady beamed.

Over our starter and mains, we conversed on everyday subjects such as the weather and the attractions of our holiday resort. She was easy to talk to – didn't continually go on about her disorders or the inconveniences which life presented. She was interested in me; asking questions about my profession and passions. I found myself talking easily and without restraint. Occasionally, I noticed Christina as she breezed in and out of the dining room, clearing away or bringing out fresh jugs of water. We made eye contact once and she winked at me. I felt my heart melt into a gooey mess and completely lost the thread of my story.

"Err... Oh dear! I've forgotten what I was saying." I confided.

My old lady beamed.

"This happens to me all the time, but I put it down to old age – this shouldn't be happening to you quite yet! You were telling me about an art exhibition you attended."

"Oh yes!"

We continued to talk until our desserts appeared. Christina, I noticed, took the dishes from the waitress and brought them over herself, which I thought was rather unusual.

"Is everything alright at this table?" She asked pleasantly.

"Oh yes, dear." My old lady enthused. "This young lady has been so kind as to keep me company and I have very much enjoyed my dinner, thank you."

I watched as she spoke. Her hands were placed in her lap and her shoulders, hunched, making her look even smaller. With each word, she bobbed a little; up and down in her seat – almost like an excited five-year-old.

"...And this looks lovely! What a treat!" She remarked, as she looked at the apple crumble and custard before her.

"I'm so pleased, Mrs. Bonner. Please enjoy the rest of your stay." Christina then, turned to me. "Is everything ok, Kat?"

She gave me a meaningful look.

"All good." I replied.

"I'll be in the office later, if you want to talk..."

"I was thinking of having an early night." I replied, apologetically.

"It will do you good. I'm not around tomorrow during the day, but I'll catch up with you, perhaps in the evening?" She suggested.

I nodded my agreement.

"Have a good evening, ladies." She said and squeezed my shoulder.

"Thank you, dear, and good night."

"Goodnight, Christina... And thank you for all your help, today." I added.

Christina made no reply but gave me one of her heart rendering smiles. I took a deep breath as she walked away from us.

"You seem like close friends. Have you known each other long?"

Christina left the dining room and I allowed my attention to return to the old lady.

"Only since Saturday."

"Goodness! I'd have said at least ten years!"

I laughed.

"We have a lot in common and she has been extremely kind to me. I am here with my Aunt, who can be, let's say, a little troublesome. Christina also has an aunt here, and when the two old ladies get together... Well, it generally means trouble!"

"Oh! Goodness me. I do hope it hasn't ruined your holiday?" She replied anxiously.

"It has rather."

"Do you mind if I make an observation?" The lady asked, politely.

"Please do." I replied, tentatively.

"You may have noticed that elderly people - especially females, have a tendency to ask impertinent questions, and get away with it." She chuckled mischievously. "When I walked into the dining room this evening, I noticed how sad and far away you looked. I do hope your troubles will be of a short duration."

I smiled but tears filled my eyes. Was I so transparent? A complete stranger had walked into a crowded room, full of noise and bustle but had noticed that my life was in tatters. She stretched out her knobbly, old hand and rested it on top of mine. It was warm and comforting.

"You know, my dear, in life, troubles come and go and as hard as we try to avoid or ignore them, have a way of intruding like meddlesome old women who are wearisome and irritating. And the easiest way to conquer your adversity is to embrace it face to face. Your dilemma today will become tomorrow's ashes, from which your happiness will grow."

Her profound words filled me with hope and resolve for the future. My life might now be in shreds, but tomorrow and the next day and the day after that, it will be different. I, Katherine Rider, will not allow Aunt Phoebe, Jilly Gerard or any other adversary, to grind me into the mud like a used cigarette butt. I will fight back; I will make the best of my life and I will not complain. I am still me and my family, still my family. Nothing has changed.

"I don't even know your name."

"It's Edie - Edie Bonner."

"May I call you Edie?" I asked.

"My dear... Of course you may!" She cried, delightedly. "You've been kindness itself to me this evening, but if you will excuse me now, I will retire to my room. I'm feeling a little tired."

As she spoke, she rose from her chair and I did likewise.

"Edie... Thank you for... for everything."

She smiled at me and touched my cheek.

"Good night, my dear and God bless you."

And with this, she turned and walked slowly out of the dining room.

Chapter 18

My night's sleep had been better than I supposed it might. I was emotionally drained, but now had a glimmer of hope for the future. I knew my life with Jilly was fast coming to its conclusion but at least from here, I would no longer be living a lie or feeling the brunt of her temper. I didn't hate her – I just didn't care for her any longer. We had out-grown each other, but until this week, I had not realised it. It was time to move on - to make a change.

Yesterday had been a revelation in itself. My Aunt was my birth-mother and my beloved parents, technically, my Aunt and Uncle. This had been hard to accept, but at the end of the day it really didn't matter. I loved my parents to bits and regardless of whose seed had been planted into whose womb; they would always be my Mum and Dad.

Mum was driving down this morning and I longed to see her. I could picture her now – an anxious face, eager to sooth her eldest child in her hour of need. My instinct was right. As her car pulled into the car park at the rear of the hotel, I could see she had slept badly and was worried sick. I needed to push away that anxiety as quickly as possible. I hurried down the staircase and through the hotel reception. The young girl on the desk eyed me curiously as I ran past and out into the open to greet my Mum like a five-year-old after school had finished for the day. As we met, I flung my arms around her, squeezing hard. She squeezed me back; our embrace demonstrating our devoted, mutual affection for each other.

"Oh! Kat!" Mum cried, through her tears. "I'm so sorry."

"Mum! Stop it! There's no reason for you to apologise. What's done is done. We move on now, ok?"

Mum nodded her agreement and we both laughed through our tears.

I hadn't seen Aunt Phoebe that morning. I was beginning to feel some concern and said as much to Mum. We decided to venture to her room together – Aunt Phoebe may have been my birth-mother, but she was Mum's sister and had been for a hell of a lot longer! So I reasoned, therefore, that she was still Mum's responsibility, and not mine... Yet!

I tapped lightly on the bedroom door and waited for a command to be boomed out in my Aunt's usual manner... There was only silence. Mum looked at me and raised her eyebrows.

"Maybe she's downstairs in the lounge." I suggested.

"We'd better go and see."

As we got to the bottom of the stairs, I caught a glimpse of Christina, laughing with someone in the little office behind the reception desk. Her companion's laugh was deeper and not one I recognised. It was a man's laugh – the only male who worked at the hotel was young Ryan but he was a lean, spotty youth whose voice had hardly broken.

"Where's the lounge?" Mum enquired.

"This way."

I indicated towards a glass, double door along the corridor, but before we took another step, Christina stepped out of the office. She was immaculately dressed in light, summery clothes with strappy sandals – she looked adorable! My heart stood still for a moment – I was breathless...Until Martin James stepped out beside her, equally dressed to impress. When I had met him at his bistro, I hadn't realised what a handsome man he was. I suppose at that time, my mind had been full of my own problems and in truth, had hardly given him a thought. He was tall and dark, with chiselled features – he could have been the next '007'. He smiled broadly at me and offered his hand, to shake.

"Hello, Kat. Lovely to see you again. How are you?"

I glanced at Christina who had already fallen into conversation with Mum.

"I'm well, thank you. You look very smart."

This was all I could think of to say at that moment. My mind was attempting to process the situation before me. Christina turned to me brightly.

"Morning, Kat. How are you?"

"Fine, thanks. This is my mum, Stephanie Rider."

I felt foolish saying this, after all, Christina had just been in conversation with her and I'm sure Mum would have explained her standing in the family.

"Yes, we've met." She replied, smiling her gorgeous smile at my parent. "You know Martin, of course?"

"Yes."

"We're visiting Martin's parents, today, so I won't be back until later. Will you be staying over, as I'm sure we can find you a room, Mrs. Rider?

Huh...Visiting Martin's parents!

"Thank you, love. That's very kind of you. I was hoping to be going home later today but I need to get one or two things sorted out first."

"That's no problem at all. Our receptionist for the day is Grace." She said, turning to a young girl in the little office. "She will organise a room for you and will ensure you have everything you need. Well, it's been lovely meeting you, Mrs. Rider and I hope you enjoy your stay with us."

Christina turned her attention to me again...

"I'll probably not see you until tomorrow, Kat. Hope you have a lovely day."

And with this cheery farewell, she glanced up at Martin, gave him a beaming smile and the couple walked out of the reception together, arm in arm, like two famous movie stars at an awards ceremony.

"What a stunning looking couple." Mum observed. "Engaged too!"

"No!" I cried in alarm.

"Well, I think they are about to break the news to his parents."

"What makes you think that? They aren't an item!" I answered resolutely.

Mum frowned.

"Well, that's not the impression she just gave me. She was wearing the ring and everything!"

I turned to my mother in shock and disbelief. Surely, if Christina had been engaged to Martin... or even seeing him... wouldn't she have mentioned it to me? She had only ever mentioned an ex-partner who she had lived with in France. The first time Martin had been mentioned by Christina was on the day we visited his establishment. Surely Mum had got it all wrong... Hadn't she?

"She as good as said that they were going to announce it to his parents over lunch."

For the third time in one week, my world turned upside down. I was lost to Jilly; my Mum wasn't my real mum, and now, the woman who I had fallen in love with was becoming engaged to 'James Bond'! How was I to cope with everything? I felt myself paling with every, passing second and I was beginning to see stars as the room around me turned black...

"Kat! Come on honey. Wake up!"

From somewhere, I could hear a voice... Mum's voice, but I was in a dark, cosy, safe place and really didn't want to be disturbed. But Mum was persistent and continued to pester me back into the real world. I moaned as I reluctantly came around, not realising where I was or why I was there... until the light of day and my new pain hit me.

"In the old days, I would have carried smelling salts with me."

Without looking, I knew Aunt Phoebe had materialised. She was the last person I wanted to see at that moment.

"I have some!" Another voice joined in. It was vaguely familiar but I couldn't focus on the owner.

Suddenly, a powerful blast seemed to explode in my brain - it brought me back, well and truly into the real world.

"Oh God!" I exclaimed.

"That's better!" Aunt Phoebe uttered gleefully. "Always does the trick."

"You ok, love?" Mum asked, anxiously.

"Yeah... I'm fine. What happened?"

"You blacked out."

I blinked, bemused. Passing out wasn't my usual thing. I took a look at the various staring faces who looked on, but eventually, focused on the old lady who I'd met in the hotel dining room the evening before. She looked concerned but smiled sweetly as our eyes met.

"I hope you are feeling much better now, dear?"

"Yes, thank you. I'm just sorry to have been such a nuisance."

"You haven't been." She replied sweetly before turning and leaving us alone.

Chapter 19

Aunt Phoebe asked for coffee and biscuits to be brought into the garden. Mum found a shady spot and we settled down... ready for battle.

My thoughts were rather scrambled. I did start to wonder if this was all a horrible dream and I would, at any moment, wake up, safe and sound and in my own bed... No such luck... Aunt Phoebe sat glaring at me as mum looked on with compassion. She drew her weapon and prodded me viciously.

"I'm not sure why your mother is here, Katherine. It seems such a shame to have made her drive all this way for nothing. You need to grow up, young woman!"

"For nothing?" Mum exclaimed taking out her rapier and poking back. "I don't call this issue a 'nothing'!"

"Don't be ridiculous, Stephanie! You are always so melodramatic! She had to learn the truth one day, so why not now?"

I suppose in retrospect; my Aunt spoke the truth. I did need to know about my past but I would have endured it better had it been explained tactfully and tenderly by Mum... The bull-in-a-china-shop tactics which my Aunt specialised in, had not been welcome.

Mum raised her shield.

"Because she is my daughter and I had the right to explain to her, but only when I thought she was ready."

"And when might that have been, pray?"

Aunt's sarcasm caught Mum unaware and she shifted uncomfortably.

"In good time." She muttered.

This left her vulnerable to the on-coming blow from her opponent.

"She's not a child requiring your protection, Stephanie. She's a woman with a life of her own. What if I died and you fell under a bus and perished? She would never have known the truth. She had a right to know!"

"Of course she had a right to know but I had a right to tell her in my own, good time..."

Mum's response knocked Aunt off guard for a moment... She remained silent, but vigorously brushed straight, a kink in the table cloth.

"And of course I made provision for Kat to be told if something happened to me, years ago... A letter was lodged with my solicitor! I'm not entirely stupid, Phoebe!" She retorted, angrily.

The sisters were at close quarters but still wielding their weapons.

"Look!" I butted in. "What's done is done. As far as I'm concerned, I am still your daughter, Mum, and Aunt Phoebe is still my aunt. Nothing has changed!"

"Except when I die, you will become a very wealthy woman!" Aunt Phoebe announced.

In all the fuss, I had forgotten the properties I was to inherit and the need for procreation.

"And why is it so imperative that I have children, Aunt?"

"Children?" Mum frowned.

My Aunt carefully picked some imaginary fluff from her dark skirt; playing for time.

"Phoebe!" Mum boomed. "Answer!"

I jumped. She didn't often raise her voice and I had never heard her use this tone with Aunt Phoebe before. Phoebe looked up, resolutely.

"She needs to have a child to inherit, Stephanie. It's as simple as that."

But Aunt's reply wasn't cutting it with Mum.

"And what if she doesn't want a child?" Mum pointed out.

"Of course she wants a child! Every woman wants a child!"

"You can't make assumptions like that, Phoebe. Things have changed. She has a life of her own and even though you pretend not to understand her circumstances, I'm bloody sure you actually do! Do you really want her to go through all that just so she can inherit some rotten old properties left to you by your... your lover?"

"How dare you suggest this?"

But Phoebe's outrage left her open and mum lunged forward.

"Well, he was, wasn't he? Let's be honest here... You saw him often enough when Tom was so ill! It wasn't an innocent walk in the park you took, was it?"

I was beginning to feel like piggy-in-the-middle. The sisters had locked horns; neither giving an inch.

"By the terms of the Will, she needs to have a child to inherit. I want her to inherit otherwise the properties will end up in the hands of the State and I'm not having that!"

"Phoebe! This isn't the nineteenth century! Women aren't used as baby makers anymore for inheritance purposes!"

"It's got nothing to do with that, Stephanie. I want her to have something of worth. I want to be able to do something for her." Aunt Phoebe's voice softened suddenly. "I've done nothing for her throughout her life – the only decent thing I ever did was to give her up for adoption to you, my dear sister. She has grown up into a kind, considerate and decent human being with you – something that would never have happened if she'd stayed with me."

Mum and I glanced at each other.

"If she inherits, Stephanie, she will want for nothing for the rest of her life. It will open doors to her that ordinary life can't."

Mum sighed. I think Aunt Phoebe had won the bout and she lowered her weapon accordingly.

"And I believe these days that they can do magnificent things for same sex couples who want children." Aunt continued.

I was speechless! My jaw must have dropped because Aunt Phoebe lifted my chin with the palm of her hand, placing it gently back into place.

We were all silent – each with thoughts of our own. I'll admit that the idea of financial independence was appealing – especially now as my life had fallen apart around me. I would be able to go back to studying art by visiting all those marvellously, expensive places which, aren't always accessible to an ordinary wage packet. I could keep one house as a holiday home and visit and sketch to my hearts delight, but sell the others and live on the proceeds. I would meet new and exciting people and perhaps one day, meet someone to share my life with. My heart gave a little jump as I thought of Christina – lovely, gentle, caring Christina. I had lost her forever to someone who I hoped would love and cherish her as much as I would have done.

Mum removed her glasses and rubbed her eyes. She looked tired and somehow, older. This indirectly was my fault. She looked over at me as if reading my thoughts and sighed.

"Well, of course it's up to you, Kat, but don't forget, to raise a child alone is a difficult thing. They aren't dollies that you can put away in a cupboard until you want to play with them again – it will be a human being who, for the first eighteen years of their life will demand your complete attention."

"But will also be company and comfort to you in your old age!" Aunt Phoebe added.

Children had never come into the equation – I'd never been maternal; cooing and gar-gar'ing over tiny, grizzling babies or noisy, rampaging five year olds who never get tired, wasn't my thing, and Mum's argument was convincing me with each passing moment that to be lumbered with a brat for the next eighteen years just wasn't in my game-plan.

"Company doesn't bother me, Aunt."

"It will when you get to my age!" Phoebe retorted.

"Phoebe! Stop blackmailing the child! You shouldn't have children to comfort or keep you secure in your old age."

"Spoken as someone with children!" Her sister huffed.

"Look, if Kat decided to have children, it would be because she wanted them and not for her own financial or emotional conveniences! I know her better than that!" Mum said, looking at me proudly.

...Perhaps she hadn't read my mind.

Coffees were served by an aging waitress who must have been at least eighty-five if she was a day. She was completely dressed in black apart from a white, starched, frilly apron and hat. Her facial features were lined with age and her eyes misted by cataracts. She belonged to a bygone era when serving tea or coffee was a delicate and refined business. The blue pottery mugs in which the hotel always served coffee, had been commissioned from a local potter. They were stylish for the modern day, but looked completely out of place on our waitress's silver tray. Elegantly shaped, cream coloured coffee pots with matching cups and saucers would have suited better.

She walked slowly towards us, narrowly missing a table occupied by a young, smart looking couple who were non-residents.

"Pardon me." She croaked as she swerved to the left of the gentleman's shoulder.

He ducked, instinctively to avoid making contact with the tray of goods and his lady gave out a little cry.

It was with more luck than judgement, that the tray made contact with our table. It rested haphazardly on the edge as she served us, but I kept a keen eye open, making ready to support it should it begin to tip.

"Have you everything you require?" she asked, courteously.

"Thank you."

The waitress nodded and picked up the tray. As she turned, I heard her mutter something before teetering away with the empty server. The gentleman at the next table ducked automatically as she wobbled by; probably expecting to be brained by the tray.

I pressed my lips together; attempting to smother a giggle, but the harder I tried, the worse it became until I exploded with mirth and the cares and woes of the last few hours seemed to evaporate into thin air. Mum smiled and started to chuckle. Half expecting Aunt Phoebe to remonstrate with us, I was pleasantly surprised to see her smiling, instead. The little tableau had lightened our situation and suddenly, we were a family again.

Chapter 20

I spent most of the afternoon by myself. Mum had taken Aunt Phoebe down into a nearby seaside town in hopes of buying suitable ladies underwear of a certain quality, leaving me to my own devices.

I took a stroll down to the sea front and ambled along a little way, watching the sea sparkling and foaming as it's rolling waves crashed onto the shore. It hissed and sighed as it settled then, receded, dragging some of the smaller stones in its wake. Small children ran around, screaming with delight as they made sandcastles – or, in my opinion, excuses for sandcastles! Nothing could have rivalled the complex fort-like extravaganzas which Dad, Anna and I constructed... Well, in truth, it was really Dad – he spent hours scooping out damp sand with a child's yellow-handled spade, lovingly fashioning it into a moat after building up the castle defences. Then, just before the tide trickled in filling the moat with sea water, would place a Saint George's flag of England into the highest castle turret. Anna and I would cheer and Dad would stand back with hands on hips, to admire his handy work.

"A castle that any great King would be proud of!" He'd boast with a smile.

We didn't doubt it!

I smiled too, at this memory. I loved my Dad – even if he wasn't any blood relation to me, I loved him very much. As a child, he'd spent hours with me, explaining homework, fixing bikes, building go-carts, teaching me to draw and keeping me safe. As a young adult, he listened to me, advised me and steered me in the right direction. He huffed and puffed a little when Mum told him that I preferred girls to boys, but after the initial bombshell, resigned himself to the fact and seemed to enjoy the interaction with my subsequent girlfriends to any of the boyfriends that my sister brought home.

I was still deep in thought when someone on the beach shouted 'Christina'. It shook me from my cosy reverie and I looked about, half expecting, half hoping to see my Christina walking along the promenade towards me. However, on this occasion, Christina was a small dark haired girl of about two years old, toddling around on the sand in a sagging nappy, clutching an over-sized bucket and spade and wearing a huge smile. Life was good for her.

Of course, my Christina was being wined and dined by her future in-laws. My heart pounded with regret for the love I could never have. But this feeling of sadness was short-lived as a small voice called to me from nearby.

"Hello Katherine, dear."

It was my little old friend from the hotel. She was sitting alone on a promenade bench – watching the world go by. I was pleased to see her friendly face beaming from the seat. I walked over to join her.

"Hello, Edie. What a lovely day again."

"It certainly is dear. How is your mother?" Mrs. Bonner enquired kindly.

"Very well, thank you. She has taken my Aunt into town to buy some bits and pieces. I must admit that it's nice to have a break."

"And then, I call you over and you're stuck with another old biddy!" She chuckled.

I laughed too.

"Not at all. Isn't it wonderful?" I said, indicating to the antics on the beach.

"Oh yes! I love watching the little children... And some of the bigger ones!" She said, pointing her gnarled old finger towards a group of teenagers frolicking around in the sea. "Sometimes they are funnier than the tiny tots!"

We watched together - silently for a while... I got to wondering about what it would be like to have a child. Perhaps my Aunt was right... A child could be company for me in the long term and the money would certainly help. Then suddenly…

"Money isn't everything, you know. It can be useful, but it's better to be happy with nothing."

How odd! It was as if she'd been reading my mind!

"Don't be lured by 'forces', into what isn't natural to you. Be true to yourself, Katherine Rider… always."

I wasn't sure what to say. I watched her rummage in her handbag, and taking out a paper tissue, gently dabbed the corners of her mouth. She placed it back into her bag and turned to me. I laid my hand over hers and squeezed it gently.

"Bless you, Katherine. You're a good girl. I wish you all that is good in life, my dear."

And with this, she rose stiffly from the bench and ambled away slowly.

I watched her progress along the promenade and wondered if I should go after her, but something, I know not what, held me back.

I arrived back at the hotel – Mum and Aunt Phoebe were still out and apart from some elderly residents snoring in armchairs in the lounge, it was very quiet. I took my sketch book out into the garden, and finding a comfortable seat with a view, did some rough drawings of my surroundings. Suddenly, my phone rang. I fished it out of my bag and was surprised to read Jilly's name on the display.

"Kat! Is everything ok? I haven't heard from you in days and I've left dozens of messages for you!"

I hadn't checked my messages for a while – I'd had one or two distractions to fill my time.

"Sorry, Jilly. It's been pretty full-on here." I apologised with a sigh.

"It is tomorrow you're coming home, isn't it?"

Her voice was gentle. I hadn't heard her speak like this for some time.

"Yes. I'm looking forward to getting back."

"I'm looking forward to it too."

I frowned. Jilly didn't do 'fluffy' but 'fluffy' was her mood at that moment.

"I'll plan a lovely dinner for us – a welcome home dinner!" She announced, happily.

Oh no! Jilly's dinners were famous – infamous, really... She'll invite all her fancy friends when all I want to do is to clamber into a lovely, hot bath and soak.

"Please don't go to any trouble. I don't think I want a lot of fuss and people."

"No! Just you and me... Like in the old days, Kat. Cosy and candles!"

This surprised me... greatly! I couldn't remember the last time Jilly and I had shared an intimate dinner for two.

"Oh... Ok, but a sandwich will be fine."

"Indeed it won't! That isn't good enough for my darling."

Hold on just a cotton-pickin' minute! Her 'darling'! What was this?

"I have missed you, Kat." She added, sadly. "I know I'm not always as appreciative of you as I should be, but when you're not around, the place is so empty and quiet... And lonely."

Her words were spoken genuinely – or so it seemed at that moment. I reserved judgement.

"Give me a call just before you leave – that will give me an idea of what time you'll be home."

"Ok." I replied, uncertainly. "Are you alright, Jill? You sound... I don't know... Perhaps a little down?"

There was a silence at the other end of the phone before she spoke.

"We'll talk about it when you get home. Don't forget to call me tomorrow, will you?"

"I won't."

"Enjoy the rest of the day."

"I'll try."

"Love you, Kat."

This was the first time Jilly had told me she loved me, in goodness knows how long... What could I say to her in return?

"Jilly... I can't hear you! The signal isn't great! If you can still hear me... I'll see you tomorrow!"

And finished the call.

I felt mean, but I didn't know what to say to her. I felt differently now – liberated somehow, but deep down inside, I didn't want to hurt Jilly. She had made my life difficult at times and we hadn't been happy for a long while, but it hadn't always been like this - we had enjoyed some fantastic times together.

I had to end this relationship. Oh crikey!

Chapter 21

Mum and Aunt Phoebe spent most of the day together. They hadn't done this in years and it was good to see them as proper sisters rather than mere siblings. The age difference between them was great and had always given the impression of being a mother and daughter relationship. When they arrived back at the hotel, they were chuckling.

"What's so funny?" I asked as they entered the lounge.

"I don't think you want to know!" Mum grinned.

This of course was red rag to a bull.

"Of course I want to know! Do you want a cuppa? They are serving afternoon tea, at the moment."

"Oh tell her, Steph!" Aunt Phoebe cried.

"Shall I?"

"Tell me what?" I asked with a frown.

They glanced at each other and giggled like naughty school children hiding guilty secrets from their parents.

"We've booked a holiday!" Mum whispered.

Aunt Phoebe looked at me and she raised her shoulders until they rested under her ears and tittered.

"A holiday?" I enquired.

What was so funny about booking a holiday?

"Your mother and I have booked a holiday in Thailand!" Aunt Phoebe announced, proudly. "We'll be away for three months…"

"Thailand? Three months!" I yelled.

"Shush, Kat!" Mum laughed. "We don't have to let the whole hotel know!"

"Why bloody Thailand, for Heaven's sake?"

"It's a place I've always wanted to travel to and explore." Aunt Phoebe explained.

"Yeah, but what about Dad?" I asked, turning to Mum.

"Oh, he'll be fine." Aunt Phoebe stepped in.

"Mum?" I questioned.

"I've spoken to your Dad and he was fine about it."

I looked at her doubtfully. I'd never known my parents take separate holidays and this new scheme seemed like the first steps in a marriage breakdown.

"He said it will give him a chance to do some work around the house without me getting in his way and moaning about the dust."

I sat bemused. My Aunt was in her eighties and mother in her sixties. Here they were, casually announcing, they were going on an adventure holiday together, in Thailand – a place perhaps, best avoided by ladies of a certain age when not accompanied by an experienced male escort.

"You do realise some of the things that go on in countries like Thailand, don't you?"

Suddenly, my role had changed. I now donned the hat of a 'parent' and all the emotional baggage which accompanied it when dealing with over-enthusiastic teenagers all set to embark on their first two-week package holiday in Lanzarote... Except I wasn't dealing with teenagers – I was dealing with adults; two rather respectable adults who should've known better at their respective ages than to want to trek about places which shouldn't attract them in the first place!

"Oh things happen in all countries, Katherine. Why would anyone want to interfere with two old women like us?"

"Not so much of the 'old', Phoebe!" Mum corrected.

"They will interfere with you, Aunt, because you are who you are! Two vulnerable, older women, travelling around with no escort. You were made for interfering with!"

They laughed! They just sat there and laughed at me! Rocking with laughter... or so it seemed. I was beginning to feel rather irritated.

"Well, ok... You two might think this is going to be a huge adventure, but I'm not so sure!" I hissed angrily. "I just can't believe you would do something so stupid and... and irresponsible at your ages..."

"Why do you keep referring to our ages, Katherine? We're not children!"

I'd run out of argument and puff. I just wanted this day to go away and leave me in peace. I wanted to wake up at home and find this awful week had been just a dream. Did I really deserve all this?

Mum rested her hand on mine.

"We'll be alright, Kat. The lady in the travel agency has arranged everything for our enjoyment and safety. We know exactly what we'll be doing and where we are going each day – look... I have a copy of the itinerary." Mum said, holding up a folder.

I sighed, heavily. As usual, I was beaten down and had to accept the situation. I shrugged my shoulders in surrender and Aunt gloated.

"Now maybe we can enjoy our tea and cake in peace without you getting in a state over nothing."

"I think we should leave it there, Phoebe." Mum warned.

"Good afternoon, everyone! How are we all?"

We looked up as Christina stood before us in her usual, cheerful way. My heart thumped as always when she was near, but somehow, I felt irritated too. Why should she be so happy and smiling when I felt like shit? Why was life always so good for some people?

"We're very well, thank you dear." Aunt Phoebe answered for us all. "My sister and I have just booked an adventure holiday!" She announced, proudly.

"How lovely! Where are you off to?"

"Thailand!"

There was a deadly silence from my friend. She glanced at me and then at my relations in turn.

"Thailand? Really?" She asked, looking back at me in astonishment.

"Nothing to do with me." I said, raising my hands in defence.

"Ok. Well, I hope you have a marvellous time!" Christina smiled uncertainly. "We wondered if you might like to dine with us this evening. My Aunt is going home tomorrow and has asked specifically if Mrs. Rider and Mrs. Hawkins could be of the party."

"That's very sweet of you, Christina." Mum smiled. "Thank you."

"You're back earlier than I expected." I observed.

"Yes... Perhaps we can catch up a bit before, Kat? I'd like a quick chat about something." Christina suggested.

I nodded... My heart sinking.

I left mum and Aunt Phoebe finishing tea and returned to my bedroom. I looked at myself in the mirror and saw the face of a miserable, middle-aged woman. I had only left home a week ago and my family, lover and friend had managed to reduce me to this state. I was tired of all this... the worm was turning.

I grabbed my suitcase from the bottom of the wardrobe and taking my clothes from the chest of drawers, packed them away ready for leaving. If it wasn't for the others, I would have gladly left for home at that very moment - not sparing the horses!

A sudden knock at the door made me jump. Christina stood in the doorway with an open bottle of Shiraz.

"Hi." She smiled – a little sheepishly, I thought.

"Hi."

"I've brought this." She indicated by waving the opened bottle of red in the air. "May I come in?"

I stepped aside. At this moment in time, my heart should have been jumping for joy at the prospect of an hour in Christina's company, but sadly, I didn't feel this way. Christina was not to blame. She had never indicated any particular affection for me, other than friendship, but I'd allowed myself to become attached and now, it felt like betrayal.

She walked in and placed the bottle and two wine glasses on the little table by the window. She poured out the wine and handed me a glass.

"Good times." She toasted.

I raised my glass letting it barely touch hers.

"So... have things settled down now?" She asked as she sat on the edge of my bed.

I stared into my glass and wondered how the hell I could condense everything down into a few short sentences.

"Yes... We seem to have sorted everything out now. Did you have a good day?" I asked; changing the subject.

"Err... Yes. Very nice, thanks. You seem... A bit edgy?"

"Just looking forward to going home." I said avoiding her eyes.

"Kat?" She said, touching my hand. "What's wrong? The light has gone out of you. I hate it that you're sad."

Christina said this with such sincerity that I could have cried.

"I'm sorry. This holiday hasn't exactly worked out as I expected." I explained before disposing of a glass of red wine down my neck.

I watched as Christina re-filled my glass and waited, patiently for me to continue.

"You see, I came away on holiday with my Aunt, not expecting so many things to be happening... And suddenly, I don't know if I'm coming or going.

Christina squeezed my hand.

"I know we've only known each other a few short days, but I feel closer to you than anyone I've ever known." She confided. "It's funny how just occasionally, you meet someone and you just seem to fit together perfectly – like a kindred spirit... Or soul mate." She added quietly.

I looked for the first time into my companion's eyes. She smiled.

"I hope what I've said hasn't freaked you out too much? I know some people find it hard to talk in this way, but I believe in saying what's in my heart. I mean every word, Kat. I need you to stay around in my life."

Now, do you remember me alluding to certain females who say stuff which can be misconstrued as a declaration of affection?

"Mum said you were getting engaged to Martin."

I noticed a glow appear on Christina's cheeks. She looked uncomfortable, and now it was her turn to avoid my eyes. She was silent for a few moments before beginning again.

"Yes, it's true. We have got engaged and expect to marry next year."

"Congratulations." I remarked, grudgingly.

"Kat... I-I..."

Christina screwed her eyes up and hung her head. I felt awful. I had been mean and led her to a subject which was obviously hard for her.

"I'm sorry, Chris." I said quickly. "I was prying. Please forgive me. I think what with everything which has happened this week..."

Christina mustered her usual humour and smiled.

"Don't be silly. You had a right to know about Martin and me. We've been together for... well, it's quite a while now... Seems like forever, actually. I suppose this was the next natural step. I'm sorry I didn't mention it to you before... but I..."

"Aren't you... happy about it?"

Once again she was silent. I watched her closely.

She glanced up.

"I think you know the answer, Kat."

This is where, in all the good books, I take Christina in my arms and... But then, this was real life and not a good book. I still wasn't certain about Christina's feelings until she looked into my eyes which told me the truth.

"I'm leaving tomorrow, Christina. It will be easier when I've gone. I didn't mean to upset everything for you."

She looked up sadly.

"Oh, you haven't. You've... you've... Oh shit, Kat."

She leaned over and kissed my lips, long and tenderly before jumping up and leaving my room.

Chapter 22

I carried our suitcases to the cars. Mum was taking Aunt Phoebe home. I didn't argue. I needed to be by myself - to mull over what had happened yesterday with Christina. I knew she had feelings for me, but instinct suggested that she wasn't ready to commit to any type of a relationship - if ever. I didn't want to be the one to force her into anything... But I knew I would never feel the same way about anyone else after this. Christina was the person I wanted to share my life with – no one else would do. The touch of her soft lips on mine had secured my fidelity for good.

We all enjoyed a sumptuous breakfast of cereals and fruit, a cooked extravaganza including everything imaginable on a plate, followed by a choice of warm rolls or freshly baked croissants with homemade jam. I ate well that morning. My appetite had been somewhat sketchy over the preceding days, but now I felt much lighter in spirit – life seemed somewhat restored to a normality of sorts. I had looked out for Christina but there was no sign of her. I was equally sad and relieved. Without seeing her, I could leave the hotel and not endure the sadness of seeing her wave me 'goodbye'... maybe for ever.

The sky was grey – the first time since our arrival, one week before. My skin was bronzed and apart from some telling signs of weariness around my eyes, there was little to suggest that this holiday had been anything but splendid, when in fact; it had been an emotional rollercoaster. I closed the boot on Mum's car having secured away their luggage and took a deep breath. This was going to be the first day of my new life. It wasn't going to be an easy transition; after all, I had always enjoyed the familiarity of my surroundings and constancy of friends, relations and even lover. Obviously, I had lived a delusional life where some of this was concerned, but now, it was changing.

I kissed Mum and Aunt Phoebe goodbye, bestowing a special hug to Mum, who I'm sure, was still a little worried about me. I could read the doubt in her eyes before she drove away.

"Ring me later, Kat!" were her parting words.

I watched until their car was out of sight before turning to my own. I opened the door but before getting in, I took one last look at The Hotel Vista which had changed my life forever. Even now, I still hoped for one last glimpse of Christina, the love of my life, but if she was there, she was keeping a very low profile. I wondered (and hoped) that she was watching from a remote window and perhaps wiping a tear of regret from her eye. But this would never do! Not in my new life. 'Onwards and upwards' would be my watch-word.

I pulled into the driveway at home. Jilly's car was there; sparkling-clean as always. Jilly had a thing about newly washed cars – they gave her a real buzz. So every week, regardless of the weather or whatever we might have planned for the day, her car took priority and was taken off to be scrubbed. Luckily, she never expected me to wash her car – it was always put into the skilled hands of a guy who owned the car wash in the village. Woe-betide the rain if it happened to fall that day – she would shake her fist at the grey clouds and curse them for their watery-deluge. Usually, the clouds cleared off pretty dammed quick as if frightened of the consequences. I felt their pain!

As I walked past the gleaming soft-top, I dragged my fingertips over the newly polished paintwork just to hear it squeak. I did this, every time - It made me feel like a rebel, but I knew if I was caught, Jilly would wipe the floor with me! I wasn't to touch her car – it was a sin against the Holy Ghost! I grinned when I noticed a speck of bird's poo on the wing... Oh dear! This would cause a paddy!

I paused at the front door and pondered how I might escape the necessity of going inside... but it was too late now – she would have heard the car. I was still uneasy about the cosy, meal for two, and her sudden change of personality since I'd left home. Admittedly, there had been room for improvement, but when a relationship has failed; a certain amount of animosity is likely. I fumbled for the front door key in my pocket, but before it was found, Jilly, dressed elegantly as always, appeared. Her welcome was something to behold – certainly nothing as I'd imagined!

"Darling Kat!" She purred.

"Jilly... How are you?" I replied, tentatively.

I was a little unsure of how to continue. My experience in relationship break-ups or even, reconciliations was, to say the least, meagre!

She gathered me up into her arms like any experienced lover would, and kissed me long and passionately. I won't pretend that it wasn't pleasant – regardless of my feelings for Jilly - or lack of them, she was a tremendously attractive woman and I suddenly needed the warmth of her intimacy. So, I allowed her to bestow all her affection on me along with a jolly nice dinner and lashings of good, French wine. Two bottles later, I was certainly well and truly unable to fight off her advances and we ended up between the sheets, in what can only be described as ecstasy. The sex was wonderful and just what the doctor ordered and as I awoke the following morning, still wrapped up in Jilly's embrace, I felt strangely liberated. No more the poor, enslaved lover of this woman – I had taken from her last night but gave nothing in return. For the first time in my life, I had acted the selfish lover and I didn't care!

As I shifted, Jilly awoke and moaned quietly.

"Do you want some coffee?" I asked, in a gesture of goodwill.

"No, honey... I'll make it!" She cried as she jumped out of bed.

And I let her!

She returned with a tray laden with wonderful things and we feasted on exotic fruits and delicate tit-bits and drank fine filtered coffee. We made love again before climbing out of bed and enjoying a long, hot bath together full of bubbles made from a subtle, and I suspected, expensive bath fragrance. She washed my body gently and towel dried me with a huge, soft bath sheet.

I was beginning to lose track of myself and was in some danger of falling back into the power of Jilly when my mobile phone rang.

"Hello."

"Kat... It's Mum. You didn't call me last night – I tried ringing you, but got no answer. Is everything ok?"

"I'm fine Mum... don't fuss."

"I'm only fussing because I care, dear. I feel so responsible for the last few days, love... I just wanted to make sure you were ok."

"Honestly Mum... I'm fine. I've got things sorted out in my mind now and I know which way I'm going. And none of this was your fault, Mum. I'm only sorry that I got you involved, but I felt pretty helpless at the time, and..."

There was a pause at the other end of the phone and then, I heard Mum sigh.

"Ok. Well, you know where I am if you need me."

"Yes, Mum... And thanks."

"Love you, Kat."

"Love you too, Mum."

I ended the call and stared out of the window for a few moments before Jilly intruded upon my thoughts.

"Kat... I've been thinking... Do you fancy spending the weekend at my Sister's place?"

"What? By myself?" I asked in surprise.

"No! Both of us, silly! It will be lovely to see the new baby and I haven't seen little George and Sacha for ages. They must be growing so big now." She said, weaving her arms around my waist.

Now, if you knew Jilly well, you'd know that a visit to her sister's was usually made under great sufferance and duress. I personally liked Rachel and her husband, Geoff, but Jilly found them both lacking in the social graces and rather boring. She was horrified when she last saw Rachel and the weight she had gained since having her family.

"She's let herself go!" She'd growled unsympathetically after our last, very overdue visit.

"Well, she probably doesn't get a lot of time to visit the gym... After all, she's running around after the twins most of the time." I'd pointed out compassionately.

"In which case, she shouldn't have put on weight! No... she's allowed herself to become frumpy... And as for that lazy git of a husband... And the constant crying and screaming of the kids, gives me a headache!"

And this had incited a half hour monologue on the drawback of raising children. So why the change of heart now?

"But I thought you didn't like the children?" I reminded her.

She turned to me with her mouth open in surprise.

"You know I love Georgie and Sacha! And I just don't get to see them half as much as I would like."

I was beginning to wonder if Jilly had been taken over by some alien presence! After all, since I'd returned home, she'd been nothing but pleasant and loving and now, she was enthusing over her niece and nephew!

"... And I'd love to be able to help Rachel with the new baby! I love the smell of babies, don't you?"

Now I was really worried.

"I found a really interesting article about babies in Cosmopolitan the other day." She continued. "I've cut it out so you can read it."

"I didn't think you had any interest in children." I pointed out, hesitantly.

"What makes you think that? I love children and in fact, Kat... It sort of brings me around to making a suggestion..."

I looked up in suspicion rather than interest. Jilly moved her mouth closer to my ear and purred some words which, I thought, I would never hear from her.

"I want us to start a family! Let's have a baby!"

***

Look out for the next book in the 'My Aunt' series
The Trouble With My Aunt
Out soon!

Acknowledgements
Artwork and illustrations by Alex Ridgley and Melissa Fox.
Social media assistance by Lizzie Ridgley

Printed in Great Britain
by Amazon